A Shared Destiny

Black Victorians ~ Book 2

By

S. N. CLAYTON

Conscious Dreams
PUBLISHING

Published by Conscious Dreams Publishing
www.consciousdreamspublishing.com

Cover Design by Karen from StoryGraphicsPlus on Etsy
Edited by Elise Abram
Typeset and E-book formatting by Amit Dey

ISBN: 978-1917584432

DEDICATION

Giving thanks to The Most High for blessing me with the irresistible urge to always follow my creative passions. Nothing ventured, nothing gained!

To my mother, Joyce Clayton - thank you for teaching me to read and write before I started school. You were the one who inspired my love for books and reading, taking me to the library every week for as long as I can remember. I have this passion for reading and writing that was nurtured by your own love for literature.

May you rest in eternal peace.

CONTENTS

CHAPTER ONE

London: 1881

Georgia Claremont rushed into her tastefully decorated parlour at newly appointed housekeeper Jenny's request. Was she hearing things? The sound of a baby's whimpering assaulted her ears. Her eyes widened as she entered the room and stopped dead in her tracks.

'At last!' said Mr Daniel Henderson, the disturbingly handsome local curate of the parish. 'Take him at once, please.'

He desperately transferred the wriggling bundle into Georgia's arms, which instinctively shot out to catch the squirming, whimpering infant.

'Now, wait one minute,' Georgia protested, looking down at the strange bundle. A large pair of teary, chocolate-brown eyes stared up at her out of a round face with a full head of jet black, soft, curly hair. As their eyes met, the baby smiled and gurgled, much to Georgia's startled surprise.

Daniel's usual cool demeanour seemed to have been rattled by the little bundle. 'I knew he'd like you,' he said with transparent relief.

Georgia ignored him and walked to the seating area by the dark-grey fireplace. She settled on a plump sofa, whose fabric blended well with the warm autumnal hues of the parlour. Georgia rearranged the baby's swaddling as best as she could. To the sound of soft cooing, she turned her attention to Daniel, looking at him suspiciously. *No man should be this handsome,* she silently remonstrated. *Let alone be a curate.* Disturbed at her train of thought—and for someone she found thoroughly disagreeable and arrogant to boot—she forced herself to return to the subject at hand.

'Mr Henderson—'

'How many times must I ask you to call me Daniel? Even Celia has given in.' Celia was Georgia's best friend. She was consumed with arranging wedding plans.

Almost gritting her teeth in irritation, Georgia narrowed her eyes. 'Well, if you haven't noticed, I'm not Celia. I'm Georgia.'

'I'm well acquainted with who you are. Do I take that as an invitation to use your first name?' Daniel stated drily.

Georgia rolled her eyes.

Daniel grinned nonchalantly, unusual for him, as he was quite a serious person. Georgia was taken aback for a moment as she watched his navy-blue eyes light up his striking dark features, no doubt amused at her surprised expression.

Georgia did her best to ignore the warm heat igniting inside her and the nervous tension in her stomach. This new aspect of his persona was making her feel ... hmm... interesting.

'Daniel, will you stop deflecting and explain why you've unceremoniously delivered this swaddling child into my arms? I'm surprised you didn't leave him on the doorstep—you practically threw the poor thing at me,' Georgia stroked the baby's cheek and smiled beautifically down at him. 'Where is his mother, for goodness' sake?'

In that moment, Georgia realised the baby was an offspring of one of their baby and mother charities' occupants, Betsy O'Sullivan. Georgia had actually held him a few times since he'd been born. His mother would be leaving the home once the baby had been adopted. Earlier, they had held a luncheon for the young women who would soon move on to new pastures. Employment had been arranged for them, as well as well-to-do adoptive parents for their babies.

'I seem to remember her asking you to hold the little one whilst, I presume, she went to attend... er ... the facilities.' Georgia said. She felt her cheeks flush. Polite young ladies avoided speaking of such personal things to gentlemen. However, at nearly thirty years of age, she wasn't quite so young anymore. Curate or not, Daniel was an infamous former rake of the highest order. It meant he barely even qualified as a gentleman, she thought wickedly.

Daniel overlooked the unusual faux pas. Under the circumstances, he didn't blame her for being so blunt. The flush on her perfectly smooth, olive-toned complexion and high cheekbones was quite endearing and gave her a vulnerable air. Georgia was quite straight-talking and sharp for a woman in the Victorian era. They were quite similar in that way, which is why their personalities tended to clash at times. Not that he would ever admit it, but he liked a woman with a strong personality. He found it rather challenging. It was a change from the usual simpering women he had to deal with, whether it was the young, empty-headed, genteel ladies who subtly threw themselves at him or their middling mothers. Not that he'd had many romantic challenges since he'd become a curate and turned his life to the word of God. It was far time he'd found a wife, according to his family, but he was much too busy with the churches in his parish and the many charitable causes he supported and championed.

He sent up a silent prayer of thanks. He would make it up to Georgia somehow. He'd had no choice but to bring the child to her. He looked at her with hidden admiration as she'd taken to instantly mothering the infant. He watched as a flustered Georgia shifted her position and brushed a curly, woolly strand of reddish-brown hair out of one of her hazel-flecked, slate grey eyes. He had found her unusual eyes absolutely mesmerising when he'd first met her and still did. Daniel had noted her warm, friendly rapport with both the vulnerable young mothers and the babies, which helped put them at ease. He wished he could say the same about himself.

Although he was friendly, at times, people found Daniel's demeanour rather intimidating and serious. They always seemed surprised to discover he actually had a sense of humour, even if it was rather dry. He was actively working on his public persona—as a curate, he needed to be approachable. Unfortunately, he never had much patience and tried to avoid suffering fools gladly. As there seemed to be a plethora of foolish behaviour and attitudes amongst the general populace, and particularly amongst the gentry, this tended to hold his social skills back somewhat in terms of his parish work. It was of utmost importance to gain the support of those in the parish, especially those who had both money and influence. Many of the less fortunate needed his help, and this took the form of many resources, most importantly, his fundraising activities.

'Unfortunately, the little mite's mother never returned, and Matron refused to take care of him. As you are well aware, we're understaffed at the moment, and the mother was nowhere to be found.'

'So, why bring him to me?' Georgia raised an eyebrow and dipped her head enquiringly.

'I couldn't take him home,' Daniel expressed with horror in his dark blue eyes. 'Anyway, you'd have more in common with him being a baby, and you being a woman and ...' Daniel paused, his usually slightly swarthy skin flushed bright red upon realising what he was about to say.

'And ... ?' Georgia's tone dared him to continue, thoroughly outraged he'd think she would automatically have maternal instincts, just because she was a woman. Did he not remember that she had a business to run? During her time running the mother and baby home, she realised that many women, if they had a choice, would never have children. At the very least, they would limit the number of pregnancies their bodies were forced into carrying. It was why the mother and baby home was so vital. Abortions were illegal and considered a mortal sin by society; the process had caused many unnecessary deaths. Childbirth came with its own dangers, and infant mortality amongst the poor was high.

Daniel cleared his throat, visibly uncomfortable with what was about to come out of his mouth. For once in his life, he seemed unsure of what to say next.

Georgia rolled her eyes heavenward. 'So, let me get this right: Firstly, as a well-sought-after curate of two parishes full of simpering admirers, I'm positive you would have had no problem finding suitable arrangements for this poor child. Instead, you immediately rush over to the proprietor of a busy bookshop simply because she is a woman. Secondly, clearly, there must be an affinity for the child who is clearly of mixed heritage, such as myself—am I correct in my thought process?' Georgia enjoyed watching the usually cool-as-a-cucumber curate squirm uncomfortably under her sardonic gaze.

'You're enjoying this too much,' Daniel grumbled and sat down in one of Georgia's plump, richly upholstered armchairs.

Georgia laughed softly so as not to disturb the dozing baby. 'Serves you right.'

'I know.' Daniel groaned. 'I panicked when Matron handed him right back to me. I didn't know what else to do. Remind me why we employed that intimidating woman?' said Daniel crossly.

Georgia shook her head unsympathetically, pressing her lips together in an effort not to laugh again. 'I distinctly recall expressing some reservations about Ms

Stewart, but *you* insisted that we needed someone who could manage the young mothers, and with a firm and stern hand.'

'Are you sure that was me? Maybe it was Celia,' said Daniel hopefully and with a sheepish expression.

They both laughed quietly, careful not to disturb the babe in Georgia's arms, who did not stir.

'You know Matron's bark is worse than her bite. But she certainly will not broker any nonsense when it comes to upturning the routine of the home,' said Georgia.

'Indeed.' Daniel sighed. He placed one of his long, tailored legs across the opposite knee.

'Please help me, Georgia. I am sorry to land the problem on you, but I need to employ a man to seek out the mother,' Daniel said.

Georgia nodded. 'What was his mother thinking?'

'You will remember the adoption fell through?'

'Oh, yes.'

'Well, that complicated things. I think she might have been worried that her new position as Lady Coppington's lady's maid would be compromised.'

'Maybe she's there,' said Georgia hopefully.

'Possibly, though I doubt it.' Daniel sighed. 'Whatever the case, we'll have to tread carefully when enquiring, as we cannot allow them to find out that she has had a child out of wedlock. Discretely finding good positions with reputable families outside of London is incredibly time-consuming and complex to arrange. It would ruin the trust process between the charity and the mothers-in-need if their situations were to become public knowledge.'

'Of course,' Georgia said, nodding her neatly coiffed head of auburn coils. She shifted the child slightly, ignoring the creases being made in the full skirt of her light cotton housedress. The costume's fitted bodice showed off her womanly curves, and the grey brought out the glittery grey of her eyes.

'It should only be for a few nights whilst I sort out alternative arrangements—if I may depend on your help, of course.'

'I'll do my best. Although I warn you, I'm not exactly the maternal type. Celia would have been much more suitable had she not been so busy.'

An acrid smell wafted through the air. Georgia wrinkled her freckled, creamy, snub nose. 'Oh, dear. I think this little tinker needs changing.'

Daniel's role as a curate meant he had to put up with all manner of unpleasant smells. He often visited the members of his two parishes, who were from all walks of life and circumstances and with varying levels of hygiene habits, some of which were questionable. He usually found a way to endure it, even if he could not cure it.

'Matron gave me a bag of supplies. I think I might have left it on the side table in the passageway.'

'Fine. Jenny and I will take a look. I'm sure Celia will be agreeable to covering me in the shop before her wedding when she can. In the meantime, I'll have to get our new housemaid, Milly, to pitch in when necessary until you can hire a nursemaid or find some other suitable solution,' confirmed Georgia.

Celia, Georgia's best friend, had recently invested in the bookshop and was living upstairs in the apartments with her. Although Celia was due to be married soon, it had been a godsend at the time, as Georgia's elder sister, Amelia, had recently left their home to become a mail-order bride in America's Wild West. It had been an upsetting time for them all. They'd all attended the same boarding school and had become very close friends over the years. As Celia and Georgia were closer in age, they had become best friends. As some of the few girls of colour at the school, it had made sense to support each other against any prejudice that might be aimed at them by some of the snobbier young ladies in attendance there.

Celia and Amelia were both Black. Amelia had been Georgia's mother's first child by her Sierra Leonean first husband, who had died young. Her second husband had been a high-ranking civil servant for the colonial British government in Sierra Leone. Georgia was her mother's youngest child by the man. As a member of the gentry, he had caused a bit of a scandal in 'polite society' when he decided to marry Georgia's mother, who had been his housekeeper, especially because her mother was fifteen years younger than her father and Black.

Sadly, Georgia's mother, Grace, died from complications not too long after Georgia's birth. Her father had remarried, to her disagreeable stepmother, and retired to his small, country estate in the British countryside.

Daniel smiled. 'I'm looking forward to conducting Celia and Nathan's wedding.'

'I'm going to miss her company, especially with Amelia gone,' said Georgia. 'She's been a rock, but I'm terribly fond of Nathan, and I know he'll make her happy.'

'Indeed.' Daniel regarded her sympathetically. 'It can't be easy losing the company of the closest people to you in quick succession. At least Celia will still be involved in the business.'

'Yes.' Georgia looked down at the slumbering child. 'Well, this little one should keep me extra busy over the next few days.'

'If he sleeps like that all the time, he should be no problem. Fingers crossed.'

'And if he doesn't?' Georgia asked ominously, observing Daniel sceptically.

'I'll be in touch.' Avoiding Georgia's eyes, Daniel stood and turned abruptly, strolling in long strides towards the door.

'Coward,' Georgia called after him, watching his wide shoulders shake with laughter as he opened the parlour door.

CHAPTER TWO

'Where is that dratted man?' Georgia said through gritted teeth. She was attempting to change a squawking Nicholas's nappy without pricking his precious skin with the large needle needed to securely stitch the fabric together. Her dressing gown tie kept getting caught up in the nappy with all of the child's toing and froing and twisting.

'Let me,' Celia, pushed Georgia gently out of the way with one of her long, slender, chocolate-toned hands. 'Go and get washed and dressed. I'll take care of this adorable little mischief maker.' How glad Georgia was to have Celia restored to her company, freed at last from the endless preoccupations of her nuptial arrangements.

'Adorable?' Georgia sniffed resentfully. The slumbering darling from day one of Georgia's penance had disappeared within minutes of Daniel's leaving. 'You seem to be a natural with him.' Georgia had been driven to the edge of her patience after three sleepless nights.

Celia giggled, her large, innocent, dark brown eyes crinkling with amusement at the harassed state of her usually cool-as-a-cucumber friend.

'Stop that at once and concentrate. This isn't the slightest bit funny.' Georgia frowned at Celia, who laughed even harder whilst rocking Nicholas to comfort him.

'I told Daniel I was not maternal in the slightest—why has he left me like this? Two nights, he promised—can't he count?' Georgia grumbled as she left the boudoir area to take care of her ablutions in her tiny washroom.

They'd been using a makeshift bassinette in a drawer from a chest of drawers in the spare servants' room in the attic, but the baby hated it. Georgia was terrified to take him into bed with her—what if she crushed him? It was a vexing situation.

To Georgia's consternation and great relief, she returned to find that Celia had managed to change him. She held the gurgling baby in her lap as she fed him some porridge Jenny, their housekeeper, had prepared and brought to Georgia's small boudoir.

Feeling thoroughly refreshed from her late morning ablutions, Georgia felt thoroughly refreshed. She smiled at the picture of potential motherhood displayed in front of her. Celia would make a great mother. Her, not so much. Celia and her sister Amelia loved to coo over babies and children and always dreamed of getting married and starting their own families. Although Georgia had not been averse to it, she felt quite neutral about the subject of marriage, though she had never upheld the institution or considered a family as a major aspiration.

As a mixed-race, independently wealthy young woman living in multicultural London, it had already proven difficult to find the right type of partner in terms of class and race. The options for marriage were scarce for a young woman born out of wedlock to her father's African servant. Even though her now-retired father had been an esteemed barrister and member of the gentry, he had a notorious reputation for seducing his female servants of any race, hence Georgia's existence. Goodness only knew how many illegitimate children he had scattered about. He acknowledged Georgia for reasons only known to himself, and he rarely discussed her mother unless her sister Amelia brought her up.

Amelia had been born to her housekeeper mother during her previous marriage to the son of an esteemed local chief. She had left her father-in-law's thriving chiefdom when it was implied she should establish a union with a distant cousin she had no feelings for after her first husband had died from a short illness.

The widow met Georgia's father, a widower, after he had taken up a position with the colonial government in

Sierra Leone. He had insisted that Amelia, who had been living with her maternal grandparents whilst her mother worked as a housekeeper, should grow up in the same household as Georgia so she would not be lonely. He would also become Amelia's benefactor.

When their mother died of complications shortly after Georgia's birth, he had been devastated and moved back to England. He'd ensured they would be provided for, with the best education and lacking for nothing financially. This, in spite of society's disapproving eyes and those of their apoplectic elder brother, who had been conceived within their father's first marriage, and who was absolutely outraged at the turn of events. As far as their brother was concerned, what happened in Africa should have stayed in Africa.

Georgia and Amelia had attended Lady Ward's School for Young Ladies, where they had boarded and made firm friends with Celia. In concession to his new wife and his eldest son and heir, their father had kept them mostly away from polite society. Once they had left school, he set them up with the stationery shop, the apartments above, a housekeeper and a housemaid.

They loved their father, although they hardly knew him, as he had been warm and affectionate when they were young, but once he'd remarried, he became distant and seemed to be ruled by the iron fist of their stepmother, who was as rich as Croesus.

Georgia and Amelia's father had been overprotective of both of them until their mid-twenties, and he attempted to head off fortune hunters. Georgia was now in her late twenties, and Amelia was in her early thirties. They seemed to be well past their prime according to society's standards. Hence, the reason why Amelia had hastily travelled to America's Wild West as a mail-order bride.

Georgia longed to love and to be loved back, but she was hesitant to actively seek out the institution of marriage and leave a life where she had only herself to answer to. Neither had she felt anything but a mild physical attraction or certain fondness for the few suitors who had attempted to take her hand in marriage in the recent years.

She had grown up in elevated circles, where few people married for love. Marriage was mostly about family alliances, security and status. Georgia had never been particularly material, and if she was perfectly honest with herself, she was terrified of childbirth after learning from her awful stepmother just how ill her mother had been after her birth. It had been inappropriate to disclose the details to her at such a young age, but it was meant to deter her from straying into the arms of unsuitable suitors who might take advantage of an innocent.

Ever since her stepmother's disclosure, she had been terrified that she would die from complications derived from a difficult birth, just like the mother she had never really known.

'There you go, my darling,' Celia encouraged the baby boy who seemed determined to please her by gobbling up the healthy porridge with vigour, even if he managed to spill most of it down Celia's light cotton dressing gown.

Georgia had put on an old dressing gown over her charcoal grey and black striped costume to protect it from any baby shenanigans. 'Let me take over. You go and get dressed.'

Celia had already carried out her morning ablutions whereas Georgia's dressing had been interrupted when Celia had come to her modest apartment to enquire as to why Nicholas was wailing so passionately. Her long, jet black, coily hair had been oiled and styled into two canerow plaits along each side of her head the night before. She just needed to finish dressing and style her hair into a loose chignon, and she would be ready.

Georgia admired her friend's beautiful, nut-brown skin. Celia looked up with a large pair of thickly lashed, almond-shaped eyes. She stared into Georgia's hazel grey slanted pair.

'What's wrong?' Celia asked, puzzled by Georgia's intense examination.

'You're going to make a fantastic mother one day. You and Nathan are going to look like a royal Nubian bride and bridegroom at the wedding. I can't wait to see what my beautiful godchildren are going to look like.'

'Oh, bless you, but I fear you are biased when it comes to Nathan and I.' Celia smiled fondly at Georgia, whom she loved like a sister. She rose and tried to wipe away some of the spilt porridge from the front of her dressing gown.

'Nathan and I have agreed to start trying for a family straightaway. Neither of us is getting any younger, and we are coming to the marriage quite late in life.'

Georgia giggled.

'Oops—little ears are listening.' Celia put her finger in front of her lips.

'Don't be ridiculous, woman.' Georgia laughed heartily at Celia's silliness. She really would miss her once she had moved in with Nathan, but she was ecstatically happy for both of them. Nathan was more like a brother to her than her own flesh-and-blood, prissy older brother from her father's union with his first, aristocratic wife.

'Are you looking forward to the marriage bed?' Georgia asked mischievously.

Celia looked slightly embarrassed, but she nodded her head vigorously and laughed joyously. 'It has been quite difficult to be discreet and control our urges. I am, however, determined to go to the marriage bed as innocent as possible,' Celia said.

Georgia regarded her with narrowed eyes, cutting her eyes and kissing her teeth. They burst into conspiratorial giggles.

'Listen, my girl: I'm just about holding on to my innocence for dear life,' Celia confessed.

'Behave.' Georgia chuckled and rocked the baby, who was starting to doze off now that he had been fed.

'Does it feel different with Nathan?' Georgia asked.

'Yes, it's more ... I don't know. I can't describe it. It was lovely with Ed, but I think we were just too comfortable and familiar with each other after having grown up in the same house as children. The romance just seemed to have grown out of nowhere.

"I agree with what you said in that maybe Ed was a little bit of a rebound from Nathan, and we found the whole business of keeping it a secret more exciting than anything, but I genuinely love him,' Celia mused.

Edward, Celia's former beau, had betrayed her by keeping secrets about his grandmother's plans to push him into an arranged marriage with their childhood archenemy. Edward's grandmother, Lady Benwick, who was also Celia's guardian, had betrayed both of them by putting Edward in an awkward position when he'd been accused of rape. Little did either of them know the depth of the betrayal Lady Benwick had woven to get her way at the time.

She grimaced and drew the dressing gown around her more tightly as if to subconsciously protect herself from the memory of Ed's and Lady B's betrayal. 'With Nathan, it feels more sensual and thrilling because I'm still getting to know him, and it's all out in the open. I'm no longer being kept a secret because of my race and being middle-class rather than upper-class.'

'Ironically, in Black and mixed-race circles, especially within the African Diaspora, we are considered part of the Black elite, or the Negro Aristocracy, if the media had it their way. Yet, we're stuck in the middle of two classes and two races with the added benefit of having to constantly explain our position in this country to all of them. It's difficult to fit in anywhere sometimes,' said Georgia while shaking her head.

'Good thing we fit in with each other, then, isn't it?' said Celia, smiling.

'I'm going to miss you terribly,' Georgia confessed.

'Me, too.' Celia's eyes watered.

'You're going to miss you, too? Not me?' Georgia teased in faux outrage.

'Oh, you—you're so silly.' Celia laughed through the unshed tears simmering in her eyes. It was so typical of

Georgia, who normally preferred not to show that level of emotion.

Celia sat beside Georgia on the tiny, burgundy wine, upholstered sofa, leaning against one of the plush cushions. She held the child securely with one arm and rested her other hand on one of Georgia's tiny, creamy olive-toned, freckled hands.

'I don't want you to spend your life alone. Of course, I'll be here to run the business, even when I start a family, but you have a lot of love to give. Look at how you looked out for me after Daniel's betrayal. And then there's this little one.'

'It's hardly been a success so far, has it?' Georgia looked down at the sleeping child. Nothing was able to wake him up once he finally decided to rest his head.

'Well, let's just say it's a work in progress,' said Celia diplomatically.

'I'm scared, Celia.'

'Of what, my darling?'

'Not of being alone—I love my own company. I'm terrified of *feeling* alone and trapped in an unhappy marriage,' Georgia confessed. 'I've watched my father suffer in a loveless marriage—my stepmother is insufferable and makes him very unhappy. You know, she's the reason Amelia and I were sent away to school. To get us out from under her short, fat feet.' Georgia wrinkled her freckled nose in distaste.

Celia screwed up her own freckled nose in solidarity, having met Georgia's harridan of a stepmother, but, thankfully, only on a few occasions during their school years. She knew she had only been tolerated because she was the ward of the aristocratic Lady Benwick.

Celia patted Georgia's hand sympathetically. Georgia sighed.

'Anyway, I'm in the old maid category now. I fear my rather pessimistic, so-called witty character is no longer as becoming or mysterious to potential suitors, now that I've lost the glowing aura of youth.'

'Nonsense,' Celia retorted.

'Really? Name one suitor who has approached me in the last year. There used to be a trail of them knocking on the door at one time or asking me to dance at soirees and balls.'

'It's a moot point—when's the last time you accepted an invitation to a soiree or society ball?'

'True,' Georgia said resignedly.

Celia smiled serenely. 'What about Mr Edwards, the magistrate?'

Georgia cut her eyes at Celia. 'Do not be facetious. That old fogey is richer than King Solomon and nearly as old. The cheek of him.'

Mr Edwards, who had clearly seen the best of his youth during the Regency years, had struggled to get down on one knee and quickly given up on the first attempt. His proposal to Georgia had been made with the assistance of her clerk, Tom, holding him up straight as his stooping body and crooked white wig threatened to topple him over his sturdy ebony walking stick. Georgia imagined his whole career reflected in that walking stick. The man positively gave her the creepy-crawlies.

Celia pressed her long, slender, dark brown fingers against her cupid-shaped lips. The effort not to laugh out loud had her shoulders shaking in glee at the memory of the comical event that had taken place in the bookshop. Georgia's face had been the picture of outrage.

Georgia grimaced at the memory—she had not found it funny at all.

'You can laugh, my friend. You've fallen in love twice. I have never experienced that feeling in all my years. Even so, a marriage of convenience is not for me. I fear I am incapable of falling deeply in love.'

CHAPTER THREE

Daniel smiled happily as he watched Celia glide up the church aisle with her bridesmaids and Georgia, her maid of honour. The bridal group made a spectacular vision of sateen golds and creams, lace and billowing sleeves. They reminded him of ancient African queens, with their traditional headdresses designed by Nathan's aunt. Celia looked stunning, a true beauty dressed in dark and light shades of gold. Her bridegroom, Nathan, puffed out his chest with pride as he locked his adoring gaze on his approaching bride. As for Georgia, Daniel could barely keep his eyes off her. He struggled to concentrate on his role as a marriage officiant.

The choir sang a popular Negro spiritual in deep, rhythmic tones, bringing an extra depth and cultural energy to the occasion. They sang in the style made popular by the Fisk Jubilee Singers, who had travelled from America to tour Europe earlier in the century, only to be imitated by many a choir thereafter. It brought life to the local church, which served as the spiritual and social heart of the community. He and Nathan had been through trials and tribulations with the church elders to persuade them to allow the choir to sing at the wedding at Celia's request. It had taken a generous donation from Nathan to gain their agreement—the church elders tended to have old-fashioned views, and Daniel suspected some of those views were racially skewed. God forgive their souls.

His eyes slid back to Georgia, who had led the two bridesmaids up the aisle and was heading towards the front row pew on the bride's side, where Nathan's daughter, Elouise, had insisted upon sitting after serving as one of the bridesmaids. The other bridesmaid, Jenny, was Georgia and Celia's housekeeper and dear friend. The young Irish girl had previously worked for Lady Benwick as a lady's maid and eagerly given her notice when Celia had fallen out with her guardian.

As she glided up the aisle, Georgia strained to drag her eyes away from Daniel's intense stare. She smiled and looked at the group of wedding attendees instead. With both Celia's parents having passed away, an aunt and other family in America from her deceased mother's side unable to attend, and her paternal uncle and his wife and their large brood too busy to leave their tavern in Bristol, the lack of family on Celia's side of the family was apparent, but she more than made up for it with the crowd of friends and acquaintances eager to see her betrothed. She did have Charlotte in attendance, Lady Benwick's niece, whom she considered family and had grown close to when Celia had become Lady Benwick's ward. Charlotte was also her ex-beau, Edward Langford's younger sister, who had emigrated to Canada with his new wife.

Charlotte had attended despite her grandmother's disapproval. Lady B had the temerity to blame Celia for the falling out with her grandson, Ed, despite it being entirely her own fault for deliberately attempting to fabricate outrageous events that would manipulate Ed into marrying someone else. Ironically, Lady Benwick was an abolitionist in the days of slavery and had taken responsibility for Celia when her son-in-law, Celia's godfather, had passed away. Despite Celia's godfather having some mixed ancestry via his grandparents, Lady Benwick did not approve of class and race mixing. Her mischief had got her what she wanted, but at what cost?

Her ward, Celia, had immediately left home and no longer spoke to her. Edward had emigrated to Canada and recently met his own choice of spouse in the previous month. Charlotte was engaged to be married and had not hesitated to show her disappointment in her grandmother. Lady Benwick ended up a very lonely character, but she was too obstinate to admit to her role in her own undoing.

Celia had forgiven both Ed and Lady Benwick, although she could not bring herself to communicate with someone she could no longer trust. Ed had written to her about his upcoming nuptials to the love of his life. Though they had both moved on, they continued to correspond after Charlotte's persuasion. He had even offered to give her away, but she thought it might be taking Nathan's good nature a bit too far.

Celia was to be given away by Caribbean activist and speaker Marshal Harcourt, a good friend of Nathan's. Georgia sympathised with the fact that she had wanted her uncle, her Jamaican father's brother, to give her away, but he had not been able to escape his publican duties in Bristol. Thankfully, she and Nathan would be visiting her Black American mother's sister and one of Nathan's uncles in New York for their honeymoon, and they would pass through Bristol to visit her uncle and his Scottish-born wife and their large brood upon their return to England. She was excited to meet up with both sides of her family.

Nathan's side of the church was nearly full, with his parents and family from Sierra Leone and some who resided in other parts of England. He came from a noble merchant family, with excellent contacts and networks all over the African diaspora and in Britain, so there were also delegates from important members of the political and business elite in attendance. Nathan had also attended boarding school in Britain and, after university, had spent time as a petty officer in the Navy. He was well-travelled and educated and had many acquaintances and close friends who also attended the celebration of his nuptials.

Georgia and the other bridesmaids took their designated seats. The church had been decorated with an array of multi-coloured flowers, which filled the church with aromatic scents. An additional supply of lit oil lamps stood proudly against a background of stained-glass windows, lending a romantic glow to the usually solemn and worshipful atmosphere. Once Celia had reached the top of the pews, she hooked her hand through Nathan's solid arm. Georgia blinked her eyes rapidly, happily willing the brimming tears to stay away and trying her best not to stare at the handsome curate as he smiled serenely at the glowing couple.

'Dearly beloved," he began, "we are gathered here today ...'

Daniel and Georgia danced a waltz on the rather generous, highly polished dance floor of the modest ballroom in Daniel's large family townhouse in a prominent area of Bloomsbury. It had been a wonderful service and boutique reception, attended by close family, friends and honoured guests. Daniel had generously offered his family's townhouse for the reception. Opening up the house to the couple, whom he had grown particularly fond of over the past two years, had certainly been a change.

Georgia was making the best of her free time away from the bookshop and baby Nicholas. Georgia and Celia had hired a nanny to look after the baby, which had been one of the most stressful tasks she had ever undertaken in her entire life. It brought about a variety of bizarre, unsuitable candidates ranging from spare-the-rod-and-spoil-the-child to a woman who swore she had never smiled a day in her life and didn't intend to start any time soon, to indiscreet questions about whether there were any suitable cupboards or attics that could be used to punish a child who might be given to mischief. They finally settled on a seasoned nanny, Laurel, who had come to England from Jamaica in the British West Indies, hoping to find work with a respectable family.

'Are you going to send me to Coventry forever?' Daniel stared down at Georgia's serious face, admiring her high cheekbones and hazel-grey, knowing eyes that leant more towards the grey side on that day. Her full, slightly pink lips and sparkling eyes stood out to him, and he had always been drawn to her dry wit and spirited personality.

'I'm still thinking about it,' Georgia retorted. Noticing a few guests looking at them curiously, she fixed a serene smile on her face. The last thing she needed was to inspire gossip at Celia's wedding reception, even if she and the other guests had already tearfully waved off the groom and the glowing bride to their honeymoon in their sumptuously decorated wedding carriage earlier on. She was still vexed with Daniel for leaving her to look after the baby for longer than they had agreed due to his having to 'conveniently' leave London on 'important' matters.

Daniel's eyes continued to flutter across her face. Her maid of honour's dress exquisitely fitted her petite frame. It was a pity he had no intentions of ever marrying and preferred the quiet life of a bachelor these days. Georgia would make a wonderful wife for the right man one day. It would have been beneficial to have an intellectual, business-minded mate such as Georgia, who had more than tittle-tattle and polite society small talk to offer in a marriage. Unlike many Victorian men of his calibre, he did not find that type of woman appealing.

As he dipped and flowed through the dance, his hand firmly on her back, he took deep pleasure in the comforting sensation of her soft, delicate hand in his strong, lean one while the other rested on one of his broad shoulders. He wondered if Georgia had had any marriage proposals yet. Based on her looks alone, he would guarantee it. Daniel the Curate held his partner respectfully; Daniel the Virile Man tried hard not to focus too long on Georgia's finely shaped figure. She had an ample bosom, which had been eagle-eyed by many a gentleman admirer that day. It was hard to miss, given her small frame encased in her glamorous wedding costume. In fact, he had had to stare down a mature, regal-looking gentleman, who had been using a ridiculous pair of opera glasses to examine Georgia from head to toe. The man had flushed a harsh red when he realised he had been caught by the local curate, who, consequently, seemed no better than he at that moment. He sighed inwardly. He seemed to have no problems with self-control with other women, who constantly threw themselves or their daughters at him. However, for some reason, when it came to Georgia, it was quite testing at times, trying to battle and balance his natural, sensual instincts with his role as a curate. He felt as if he were constantly correcting himself when he was around her.

Most people who had made his acquaintance were quick to point out that he was nothing like the average curate, either with his dark, swarthy looks or his temperament, he reflected ruefully. He had never set out to be an average curate and had always just been himself, former rake or not. The scandalous stories of his rake-like behaviour coupled with his Byronic looks were enough to keep society circles in gossip for years. Despite his reputation, he had always been a deep thinker and reader and had experienced some type of spiritual epiphany whilst on a tour of Europe's celebrated religious sites. He had turned to God at a particular crossroads in his life after the years of womanising, drinking and gambling had caught up with him. His life had started to feel empty and meaningless, and his calling had come at a drastic turning point in his life, but he was not the pious, sanctimonious type of curate most people expected him to be.

Daniel had gone on to tour America not long thereafter, visiting many Evangelical and Anglican ministries and getting involved in supporting various initiatives for both the poor of all colours and freedmen still trying to rebuild their lives, as well as schools, colleges, churches and other facilities post-slavery. Particularly in the South, they were facing rising racist attacks, Black codes, and the government turning coat on many agreements. The added issues of former slave masters returning to force ex-slaves into contracts, employment laws criminalising unemployed coloured people, and the kidnapping of children to force them to work for free further complicated the plight of Black Americans. He had been deeply moved by the resilience and dignity of coloured men, women and children, many of whom were both proud of their African roots and had expressed their loyalty to America as a nation during two major wars: the American Revolution and the Civil War. Some of them had also fought for the British.

Once he had returned to England and started training as a curate, he continued to support many charitable causes and events related to raising funds for coloured people, both in Britain and in America, especially for Black sailors and freedmen initiatives. Due to his family's aristocratic connections, he had settled in the Bloomsbury area of London, where his townhouse was situated. He acted as curate for two parishes as well as a spiritual confidante for some titled families and other members of the gentry. Living in the family townhouse saved the church money for lodgings. Even as the youngest son, who was not entitled to inherit his father's estate, Daniel had been blessed with modest financial independence due to family trusts set up by his financially savvy grandparents, so he couldn't complain.

His ambition was to set up some type of boarding house for Black and Indian seamen, many of whom had experienced prejudice at other boarding houses or who were charged more than their white counterparts. It was something he had discussed with both Georgia and Celia—Celia in particular, for it was an ambition she also mirrored. But he did not see how this could happen without some generous, charitable funds to sustain it—it was challenging enough running the mother and baby home.

Daniel smiled teasingly as he swirled Georgia through the dance.

Georgia continued with her false smile and flashing eyes.

'I sent a note.' Daniel remonstrated.

'Yes, you did. Nevertheless, there was no explanation as to why you felt the need to "run away" on business and leave me holding the baby ... literally!' Georgia replied, sarcasm lacing her voice.

'I'm sorry, but my uncle is dying, and I had to see him. We were quite close when I was a young whippersnapper. I thought it better to explain in person rather than in a note, but upon reflection, maybe I should have been a little more transparent. I had no intentions of leaving you in the lurch, Georgia,' Daniel replied sombrely.

Georgia took a deep breath. 'No, it's my turn to apologise. If I'd realised, I wouldn't have treated you so coldly all day. I felt betrayed and taken advantage of. I hope your uncle recovers soon.' Georgia dipped her head to the side.

'Thank you. I appreciate the apology. Regrettably, I'm afraid my uncle is not going to recover. He's a bit of an old rascal and has had a long and interesting life, but I'm going to miss him when the inevitable happens.'

'Bless him. I know it's no excuse, but I've also been rushed off my feet with the wedding arrangements." In response to his raised eyebrows, Georgia quickly assured Daniel, 'Not that I mind, of course.'

'Some of the older guests seem to think there's an endless supply of refreshments. They're acting as if they've not eaten for months.' Georgia rolled her eyes.

Daniel laughed. 'You'd better check their pockets and purses for food. I suspect many of them are genteelly poor and just keeping up appearances.

Georgia chuckled, screwing up her face in mock horror. 'I wouldn't dare! It would, no doubt, be handbags and handkerchiefs at dawn.'

'Celia, bless her, invited some of the old dears in the parish who like to help out at the mother and baby fundraising events and soup kitchen. It doesn't help that she spent so many years acting as a companion to that mischief-maker Lady Benwick that many of the old dears in that crowd expected invites. Celia is better than me. She really is much too soft.' Georgia shook her head, smiling fondly at Celia's generosity.

Daniel nodded in agreement. He was well aware of Celia's soft spot. 'It's fascinating to watch how easily the old dears, codgers and less fortunate in the parish pull on our Celia's heartstrings.' Many of them were well-connected but had dwindling fortunes or non-existent financial security, other than a few assets on paper.

'Daniel'—Georgia laughed softly—'someone might hear you.'

'I'm jesting. I'm well aware of the situation with many of our elderly, genteel parish members. They may come from prestigious families, but they barely have a penny to their name. Then, you have some of our less prestigious middle- and working-class residents. It's actually becoming a real social issue for many.'

'Indeed. Oh, my goodness—you must think I'm wickedly selfish. I didn't ask what is ailing your uncle. Is he in pain? Am I being intrusive?' Georgia removed her hand from his broad shoulder and placed it over her full-lipped mouth in embarrassment.

The loss of her warmth left him feeling somewhat bereft, much to Daniels consternation. Before he could stop himself, he took hold of her soft, delicate hand and replaced it on his shoulder. They regarded each other, lost in the moment for what seemed an eternity. His dark blue eyes were mesmerised by her pair of glittering, hazel green orbs.

Daniel dragged his gaze away from Georgia's and cleared his throat self-consciously. A slow flush crawled up his neck and peeped atop his stark white collar. He noted that Georgia had not been unaffected: her freckled, creamy, alabaster cheeks were flushed.

'Ermm ... my uncle has been ill for quite some time and, yes, he is in pain at times. It's some type of tumour, I'm afraid. He's had a great life and is quite resigned to the fact that his time in this mortal realm is limited. But thank you for asking.'

'Not at all. It's the least I could do.' Georgia gazed at him sympathetically. 'Are you his favourite?' She smiled innocently.

Daniel watched her striking features intently. She was stunningly beautiful and intensely tempting to him in that moment. His gaze locked onto her kissable, dark pink lips. Both the bottom and top were full and begging to be kissed from his point of view. 'Something like that.' Daniel managed to answer in a low, hoarse voice. 'Is it me, or is it quite hot in here?

'Let's go outside on the balcony for a while. I need to update you on what my man has found out from our enquiries about the baby's mother.' He took a surprised Georgia by the elbow and drew her swiftly towards the open balcony door. It conveniently had a small table and two chairs placed in front of it for anyone in need of some fresh air. 'May I fetch you some refreshment? I need a drink.'

Georgia regarded his handsome, flushed face curiously. 'No, thank you.'

'Fine. Won't be a moment.'

Daniel felt Georgia watching him as he fetched the drinks from one of the waiters and made his way back to the table. He hoped she hadn't noticed his lapse in manners when he had practically manhandled her towards the table. He had tried to be gentle in his approach, and it must have seemed so to her, or she most likely would have said something. Georgia was not backwards when it came to coming forward to say what she thought. It was not a popular trait in a lady, yet it was a personality trait he appreciated.

Daniel was usually as cool as a cucumber around women, even if he was physically attracted to them. Goodness knew what was happening to him that day. He felt so much more aware of himself around Georgia. Although he had always considered her attractive, something about the softer side of her demeanour that day, as Celia's maid of honour, seemed to have sparked something within him.

He reasoned that he just needed to get a hold of himself, and he would be back to his usual cool persona. It wouldn't pay to fall for someone of Georgia's calibre. Daniel wondered who he was trying to fool.

The next morning, a weary but content Georgia sat on the floor of the makeshift nursery in her apartments and played with the baby. She missed Georgia and Nathan already and felt blessed to have baby Nicholas in her life. In the last few weeks, the little boy had grown to be healthy and chubby. He had thrived even more since they had employed Laurel, the cheerful and friendly nanny.

Laurel had gone downstairs to prepare some porridge for Nicholas whilst Georgia took some time to play with her small ward. He kept attempting to crawl back and forth on the soft blanket she had laid out on the boudoir's tiled floor. It was time to set some rules for the little one. She had given in to her fear of allowing him to sleep in her bed, as he adamantly refused to sleep in the drawer they had prepared for him, with its comfortable blankets and tiny pillow.

The baby had slept soundly every night while sharing her bed and went happily and willingly for a nap when Laurel lay him down during the day. It was time to purchase a crib and refurbish one of the rooms on the upper floor as a nursery.

There had been no sign of his mother, and Georgia was in a dilemma. She had not expected to grow that fond of him, but how could she adopt him on her own? She had spoken to Daniel about the difficulty of this—even though she was financially sound, it wasn't a usual occurrence. Though she was a woman of means, her single status made it difficult.

Those in the know were scandalised that the baby's mother had run off to get married to a wealthy widower almost double her age. When confronted by the investigator Daniel had hired, she had refused to take her son back. Her husband wanted his own children with her, and did not want the responsibility of another man's child, particularly the child of an African sailor who had no idea he'd sired a son. He had forgiven her for giving birth to a child of mixed race and out of wedlock, but he would not bring him up as his own.

The other issue was whether Georgia could manage motherhood whilst running her bookshop and seeking out other investments with her business partner, Celia. Being of mixed race, she always seemed to be judged by a different standard to her white counterparts. She had already received many disapproving glances from certain gossipy matrons in their small community of Bloomsbury and the surrounding areas connected to her charitable works.

When a titled female member of the board of their mother and baby home had taken in an African orphan girl for a few weeks before carting her off to one of Dr Barnardo's establishments, she had practically been divined as a saint. But not Georgia. She'd already had some close friends and allies come to warn her about rumours circulating regarding Nicholas's true origins. The gossip had implied that the child most likely belonged to her sister, Amelia, and that was why she had disappeared to America, and the abandoned baby story was apparently a ruse to allay a scandal.

It was unfair that even with a white father, who was a part of the gentry, she was seen as something of an unknown and untrustworthy. She had grown up with those people, for goodness' sake. Just that day, one of a small set of three harridans who had come into the bookshop merely to be nosy and spread gossip had made a comment on her situation. 'I mean, engaging in trade— how does her father allow it?' she'd whispered rather loudly to her friend, who had rather horsey features and proceeded to snort and neigh like a horse at Georgia's expense.

Georgia ignored them and sought out other loyal customers in need of her help. There was no point in putting the women in their place or overthinking the situation. She had no intention of being a part of their perverse entertainment to fill their boring, empty lives.

Goodness, look how wicked, wagging tongues could cause havoc in an innocent baby's life. What was she to do?

CHAPTER FOUR

'Suicide?' Georgia pressed her small, creamy beige hand to her full lips in shock. 'That poor girl—but why?'

Daniel shrugged. 'Who knows?'

He dragged his hand through his hair impatiently. 'It's possible she was unable to face life without the child.'

Georgia watched him quizzically. 'Is something wrong? Well, apart from this tragic debacle. You seem agitated.'

'There is something else—I'll come to that in a moment,' Daniel replied, his voice strained. 'What do you intend to do with the child?'

Georgia walked to the tall, wide, sash windows at the front of the bookshop and started dusting the books on display, her back deliberately turned to Daniel. She couldn't bear to look at him. She cleared her throat nervously. 'I'm really not sure.'

She spun around abruptly, nearly knocking the books off their display, startling Daniel and herself in the process. 'Oh, darn it. I want to adopt him—there, I've said it!'

Daniel laughed heartily, his dark-blue eyes crinkling at Georgia's clumsy admission.

'What's so amusing?' Georgia asked, smoothing the sleeve of her lace blouse with a frown.

'I practically had to get down on bended knee and beg you to take him. Now, you wish to adopt him?'

'I know,' said Georgia. 'The little sweetheart has captured my cold heart.' She waved the duster towards her lace-covered heart dramatically.

'Mm ... do you think someone else might capture your heart?'

'Like who?' Georgia's grey eyes widened with curiosity.

'Me, possibly?' Daniel leant his long body against the shop counter, watching her like a lion sizing up his prey. 'It seems clear that you need a husband and, as of this morning, I need a wife.'

There was silence for what seemed an eternity. Georgia had never truly known what a loud silence was until that moment. She forced herself to walk towards the counter calmly and started counting the day's takings. *The man seems to have lost his marbles.*

'Are you ever going to answer me?' Daniel enquired. He rested his elbows on the countertop, keeping his eyes trained upon his prey.

Georgia was determined to keep her eyes on her task. 'I'm simply waiting for you to come to your senses, Mr Henderson.'

Daniel smiled dangerously. 'So, we're back to Mr Henderson.'

'Yes, until you come to your senses.'

Daniel sighed and placed one of his rather large hands on top of Georgia's to still her remonstrations. 'I'm serious, Georgia. Do you think polite society is going to accept you adopting the child of an unwed, mixed-race mother without question and gossip?'

Georgia silently regarded his large hand as it rested on hers, transfixed, trying to ignore the sensation his heated touch ignited.

'How would it look if a single woman of child-bearing age suddenly adopted a child with no husband in tow? The rumour mongers would have a field day.

'Let's be honest: you've made a few enemies with that sharp-shooting, straight-talking tongue of yours.'

Georgia huffed and cut her eyes at him. 'They deserved it, interfering old busy bodies.'

'I'm sure they did, but does that innocent child deserve to be the centre of ridicule?'

Georgia sighed and gently pulled her hands out from underneath his light pressure. 'I never wished to be married, especially after witnessing my father's disastrous second marriage.

Georgia completed her task of putting the day's money notes, cheques and gold coins into money bags. A thought suddenly occurred to her. 'What did you mean by as of this morning, you need a wife?' Georgia asked suspiciously.

'My poor, dear uncle died this morning,' Daniel said.

'Oh, I'm so sorry, Daniel.' She ran around the counter to hug him.

Daniel smiled sadly. He returned the warm hug and savoured the feel of her petite, feminine body against his tall, lean frame. 'Does that mean I'm back in your good books?'

Georgia jerked her head back. 'This is not a time for humour.' She untangled herself from him.

Daniel struggled to wipe the amusement from his face. 'My uncle lived a very long and active life. He would want me to celebrate his life and not be morbid about it.' He looked into Georgia's hazel-grey eyes seriously. 'He's left me in a rather awkward position.'

'How so?'

'I will not inherit his estate unless I become betrothed within six months of his death. With that money, I could do many great works and support other charitable causes.'

'Six months? Daniel, stop being so dramatic. That's plenty of time. There are many a matron who would love to marry her genteel young daughter to a well-to-do curate.'

'I don't want them—I want you, Georgia.'

'Why?' asked Georgia.

Daniel shifted uncomfortably. 'I've seen a different side to you in the last few weeks. We have the same dry sense of humour and similar backgrounds. I think you'd make a gracious, intelligent wife and mother." Daniel wished he'd said that she was the most beautiful woman he'd ever known, both inside and out, but he was too cowardly to risk her sarcastic response.

'Gracious? Me?' Georgia snorted and rolled her eyes most ungraciously. 'I think you need to be aware that I am not some little innocent, Daniel. In other words, your gracious wife-to-be would not be a virgin in her marriage bed.'

Two nights later, as Georgia carried out her ablutions in her cosy boudoir, she recalled Daniel's utter shock at her revelation. His silence could have cut a knife. It was simply deadly and practically deafening compared to the earlier silence after his clumsy marriage proposal. He then walked out of the bookshop without another word.

Georgia plaited her soft, coily hair into two big canerows on either side of her head. She examined her features glumly as she moisturised her scalp with a mixture of natural oils and butters. Why had she confessed to losing her innocence in that manner? It was unforgivable, really, but she had wanted to shock him.

Gracious, he'd called her? No, I love you, you're beautiful, I can't live without you? None of the usual, romantic gestures a normal beau would expect. She knew that there was some attraction between them—she could feel it—but it was all so unromantic. Usually, that would be right up her alley—why not this time?

Georgia sighed, not ready to admit to the real reasons why she was so annoyed with his cold, business-like marriage proposal.

Georgia had lost her innocence to a Royal Navy officer who had died at sea in an accident, the result of a collision with a seafaring pirate ship from Somalia. He had been mulatto, just like herself, and her first love. She had not been ashamed or felt bad about giving in to her passions, especially once she had been told about his death. Amelia, her sister, and Celia, her closest friend in the world, had been a real comfort to her. Oh, how she needed them now, but Amelia had started her life as a mail-order bride in America's West, and Celia would be thousands of miles away in New York on her honeymoon with Nathan for at least another week.

She wondered what her deceased mother would have advised. *Go with your heart, my love.* That's what her mother had always wisely advised Amelia, and her beloved older sister had passed this on to her. Well, she had grown to love little Nicholas—could she learn to love Daniel as well?

Georgia's mother had died giving birth to her back in Sierra Leone. Their father had left them with their grandparents, who were successful merchants but quite controlling. This was the reason why their mother had taken on the housekeeper's role in her father's household once her late first husband had passed away after a short illness rather than return home. Her father was a colonial diplomat, a respectful position.

Once Georgia's mother had passed away, Georgia's father couldn't bear to stay in Sierra Leone with so many painful memories. Upon his return to England, Georgia's father had remarried to a horrible woman, who'd been useless as a stepmother and none too pleased that she had one mixed-race daughter and another coloured one. Her hostile demeanour made Amelia and Georgia feel like strangers in their own home. She had taken advantage of their father's grief. He had seemed to have almost forgotten their mother's existence.

Although Georgia knew he still loved them, she had never quite forgiven him for his emotional neglect and abandonment. Their care had been left almost completely to their governess and the house staff. It had been a relief to all concerned once they had become old enough to be sent away to a boarding school for young ladies. This is where they met the lovely Celia and became firm friends.

Georgia sat at one of the small, cushioned alcoves underneath the apartments' windows. The apartments had been lovingly decorated in shades of sky-blue, leafy-green and slate-grey, with heavy mahogany furniture to offset the lighter colours. A Japanese wall pattern, oriental rugs and majestic ornaments of blackamoors on the mantelpiece above the fireplace completed the eclectic mix. She stared out at the night sky, sparkling with stars and distant planets, wondering if Daniel had changed his mind about wishing to marry her, as she had not heard from him since his swift exit.

CHAPTER FIVE

Two days later, Daniel strolled through the neighbouring squares of Bloomsbury. He was on his way to Argyle Square to see a young girl and persuade her to take a placement at the mother and baby home, the home he had proudly set-up with the incorrigible Lady Benwick, Celia's aristocratic former guardian. It housed less fortunate souls who had no support after finding themselves pregnant with no father of the baby or prospect of marriage in sight.

The stroll through the leafy square would help him think. It was a bleak spring day, but not too chilly. Daniel wore a sharply-creased pair of trousers with a striped blue and grey waistcoat, black tie and matching frock coat. Daniel's hat sat tall upon his regal head, and his highly-polished shoes tapped loudly on the paved and cobbled streets as he strode confidently along.

He didn't dress as formally or as drearily as the average curate. As the moderately wealthy son of a baronet who was well-travelled and worldly, Daniel couldn't fit into the role of the average curate even if he wanted to. Over time, he had distanced himself from his family. They were disappointed he'd given up his political aspirations and the 'old boys' ' gentlemen's clubs to serve God.

As a former rake, it was the least they expected for him to marry well to a titled or filthy-rich heiress and secure a wealthy alliance that would strengthen the family tree. Fortunately, due to a number of trusts, inheritances and his own business acumen, he was financially secure and could choose his own path in life. This was just as well— as the youngest son, he certainly wouldn't inherit the family's estates, which was why his family had political ambitions for him.

He needed to persuade Georgia to accept his marriage proposal—how else could she adopt Nicholas without a resulting scandal stemming from pessimistic gossip within their polite circles? What better solution could there be for either of them? The child would have a respectable mother and father, Georgia would have his protection and avoid any nasty gossip, and, thankfully, he could use his uncle's inheritance to fulfil his charitable ambitions.

Ideally, he would like to extend the mother and baby home to include a small children's home for mothers and parents temporarily unable to support their families.

Daniel had never imagined himself entering a love-marriage, although he'd always wanted a family at some point. Up to then, he'd never met anyone who stirred any sort of emotional feelings within in his sensible heart.

He sighed and rubbed his chin, deep in thought. *But what of Georgia?* He and Georgia seemed to rub each other the wrong way mostly. Still, there was no denying the existence of a strong, physical attraction, and they had a similar sense of dry humour. *Wasn't that a good start?*

Daniel had been momentarily shocked at her confession. Not so much that she had lost her innocence—as a curate, he had heard it all. It was the way she had blurted out her confession. Georgia had a straightforwardness that was unnerving at times. Most men would be put off, but he found it refreshing. As a former notorious womaniser, he had never been attracted to virgins and much preferred women of experience. Interestingly, he didn't think Georgia was wanton or had taken many lovers, as she still seemed quite innocent in some ways.

Daniel grimaced slightly as he wondered who she had lost her innocence to and if she'd loved him. He experienced a surprising surge of jealousy. The same jealousy that had pushed him to leave the bookshop immediately after her confession. What was wrong with him? He had just as abruptly asked her to think things through and left.

Georgia had simply nodded her head silently, a little shamefaced. He had been in a rush the last time he had visited the bookshop to give her the bad news about baby Nicholas's mother. Yesterday, he had sent a note round to Georgia to see if she wished to accompany him to the British Museum on Sunday. It was one of her favourite places to visit, another interest they had in common. He hoped she would say yes. They could have a spot of lunch afterwards, a little courtship to further test their compatibility.

To be fair, even if Georgia *had* been wanton, could he really judge? He'd had quite the reputation as a charming rogue before discovering his faith. He hadn't lost any of his desires for an incredibly attractive woman, especially one of Georgia's calibre. He might have found God, but he was still a man in flesh, and it had been a long time since he had indulged in dalliances with any women. Daniel felt it was past time he found a wife, but not just any wife. He wanted Georgia—she was beautiful, intelligent, and she made him laugh with her straight talking and dry sense of humour. It wouldn't be a love match, but it would be the closest he could get to it in the circumstances. Maybe they would grow to love each other with God's grace.

Daniel was so deep in thought that he walked straight past his destination, Argyle Square. He chuckled to himself and turned back. For someone not in love, Georgia certainly had him acting like some lovestruck fool. As he searched for the boarding house the young, pregnant girl was occupying, Daniel hoped Georgia would come around to his way of thinking.

Daniel had a few dedicated parishioners at the two churches he served as a curate in Argyle Square. The area's decline began in the 1860s, once many of the wealthy had moved out. Most of the remaining residents consisted of the lower middle class and working classes. Sadly, there was also a semi-criminal element, and prostitution had started to creep in. So far, the church parishioners and clergy had been unsuccessful in their attempt to turn things around with some of the less fortunate residents.

Daniel stared down at the petite young girl's stubborn face and then over to the tall, stout, stern-looking features of the landlady, Mrs Wynters. They were both sitting whilst he stood in the middle of the shabby front parlour.

'Well, you can't stay 'ere. I won't 'ave it,' Mrs Wynters said.

'I've paid me board upfront for the next two months, so I ain't going nowhere,' the girl replied.

Daniel shot the formidable landlady a quelling look. She closed her open mouth angrily. Then, he turned to smile disarmingly down at the girl, Agnes Bowes. Her Anglo-Indian ancestry made her skin look as if it were slightly tanned. Agnes had been taken advantage of by her master's eldest son in their London townhouse and was now five months pregnant, though she was barely showing due to her petite frame.

Agnes blushed. Daniel was a handsome man and highly diplomatic, able to charm the most disagreeable of people in the most difficult of circumstances, which was part of his unique stance as a curate, although he didn't seem to be having much luck with Agnes's landlady. During a previous visit to the house in Agnes's absence he had tried to encourage her to persuade Agnes to see sense.

'Agnes, you'll be much more comfortable at the mother and baby home. There'll be no judgment, just support and care for you and the baby.' Daniel stared around the shabby front parlour, wondering what had happened to the landlady's fortunes, as the furniture was good quality and solid.

Agnes stared up into Daniel's striking features. 'You don't look like a vicar,' she said shyly.

'That's because I'm a curate. And, yes, I'm well aware that I don't fit into that box either. I am told I favour a first-class rogue.' He grinned mischievously.

Agnes blushed again and giggled.

Mrs Wynters sniffed disapprovingly. 'Really, Mr Henderson.'

'I'm just trying to put Agnes at ease.

"Well, Agnes, will you at least think about it? You have one month left on your board—where else can you go?'

'I don't know, mister. All I know is I don't want to give me baby away.'

Daniel nodded. 'Why don't we discuss this once you've moved in. I'm sure Matron and the home's manager will be able to seek other options for you.'

'Oh, all right ... Mr Henderson, is it? Thank you, sir.' Agnes fiddled nervously with the ends of her crocheted shawl.

'Good stuff. How about I arrange for Miss Clayborne, the home's manager, to come and talk to you about the process—does that sound good to you?'

Agnes nodded, the relief plain on her face despite her earlier obstinacy.

'Thank Gawd,' said Mrs Wynters.

Daniel shot the insensitive woman another quelling look, his blue eyes flashing with annoyance. The landlady merely sniffed and held the parlour room door open for him to leave. She'd had enough of his holier-than-thou shenanigans, and he was a little too handsome for her liking. Much too good to be true.

Daniel bowed his head to both women and placed his topper on his head. 'Goodbye, Agnes, Mrs Wynters.' He gave Agnes a discreet wink and left the room to indignant sniffs of disapproval and muted giggles.

'Why didn't you tell me they were back? I wondered why I hadn't heard from them.' Georgia clapped her hands excitedly, amusing Daniel. They had been standing in the Great Hall of the British Museum, with its mountainously high ceilings when she felt a light tap on one of her shoulders. She'd turned quickly, ecstatic to see Celia and Nathan.

'It was supposed to be a surprise.' Celia hugged Georgia joyously. Nathan kissed her hand like the charmer he was.

'Oh, how happy I am to see you two. You're both positively glowing. I've missed you so.' Georgia couldn't stop beaming.

'Well, thank you very much. Is my company that excruciating?' Daniel's dark-blue eyes sparkled with amusement.

'Oh, you ...' Georgia hit him playfully with her tiny, beaded handbag. They all laughed heartily, pleased to be in each other's company again, ignoring the discreet stares and smiles of curious onlookers.

'Hush,' Celia said. 'We'll get thrown out for making a scene.'

'Nonsense,' Georgia replied sternly. Celia chuckled.

'Well, I don't know about you three, but I'm famished. Let's go to lunch. We want to hear all about your adventures in New York,' Daniel declared.

Georgia looked at each of the friends happily as they sat around the extravagantly dressed dining table. Along with her sister, Amelia, they were all like family to her, even Daniel. She examined them, thinking what an attractive and lively group they made. Nathan and Daniel both looked debonair and handsome in their suits and tailored waistcoats, while Celia's cocoa complexion glowed against the colour of her burgundy costume and matching hat.

'Thank you, Daniel. The seafood starter was sublime.' She beamed at him, unable to hide her joy at being reunited with her closet friends in the world. Daniel smiled warmly and blushed slightly at her excited reaction to his generous gesture.

'Yes, thank you, Daniel,' reiterated Celia.

'The starters and mains were delicious, Daniel. Absolutely mouth-watering. You must allow me to contribute, my good man,' said Nathan, graciously. He smiled handsomely, showing glistening white teeth, which contrasted his almond-coloured mid-complexion.

Daniel put his hand up as if re-directing traffic. 'No, I insist. I wish to treat you both, as I had no time to get you a wedding present, and Georgia deserves a treat. She's truly been a great help, getting me out of a tight spot.'

Georgia flushed at the compliment, slightly embarrassed to be thanked in front of the group. Daniel stared at her meaningfully. Their eyes caught for what seemed an eternity. Celia coughed discreetly, and they reluctantly tore their eyes away from each other.

'Well, thank you.' Nathan and Celia exchanged amused glances, silently wondering what was going on with their friends, but they were too polite to mention anything.

Daniel had booked them a private booth towards the rear of Kettner's Townhouse, one of the most popular restaurants in Soho. It made for a chic location with its ornate chandeliers, tiled, patterned floors and heavily curtained-off private dining rooms. The restaurant's speciality was game and seafood dishes. It was a popular venue for London's elite and influential figures. Many of their clientele were members of London's creative communities.

Soho, situated between St Martin-in-the-Fields and Leicester Square, was London's largest and most easily accessible, much-loved cultural district. The Italians, Greeks, French, Chinese and many other nationalities owned eateries in the area. It was also near St Giles, a well-known, prominent Black area in the eighteenth and early nineteenth centuries.

The cosmopolitan range of cafes, restaurants and exotic characters from around the world made Soho a popular haunt for people of means, the elite, entertainers and creatives. It had originally been a popular district for the aristocracy, but was fast-gaining a reputation for being a front for London's criminal element, if one were to believe the London press.

The group of friends thoroughly enjoyed catching up during the meal. They were ready for the dessert menu and Italian coffee and biscuits to complete their dining experience.

Celia, Georgia and Nathan dined in the area quite often as it was walking distance from the bookshop in Charing Cross Road. Nathan always insisted on accompanying them. He did not trust the area's criminal element, especially the professional pickpockets, who were a constant problem in central London.

'Now that we've heard about your delightful honeymoon escapades, tell me how the race is doing in New York and other areas.' Georgia focused on Nathan and Celia, who exchanged a look.

'Well?' Georgia looked at them expectantly.

Nathan pressed his thick, embroidered cotton napkin to his lips before speaking: 'It's a mixed bag, really. Some of us are excelling in many areas of life, but many of the race are still struggling to rebuild their lives after slavery. We should have moved past the Reconstruction Era, but it's not proving easy anywhere in the country. Whether it's Black codes, segregation—especially in the South—housing discrimination, education, demanding equal and voting rights, or lynching, the list goes on, and we still have a long way to go.' He sighed heavily.

'Can you believe there's still restricted access to public and private transportation and many restaurants and other places of business in New York, of all places? Having abolished slavery long before the South, you'd think they'd be more enlightened about these things.' Celia frowned.

Daniel frowned in sympathy. 'It's a disgrace.'

Celia rolled eyes and sighed. 'Of course, it's far from perfect in London. It can be quite challenging at times, with their unspoken or blatant colour bars and discrimination, but it's simpler to navigate, especially if you have an influential network like ours. Although, admittedly, it's more complex in other areas of life: politically, education and work-wise. Just don't get me started on the state of policing.'

Nathan tutted and shook his head in agreement. 'We still have a long way to go in the Diaspora in general, let alone in Africa. It's important to support any efforts in highlighting the plight of coloured people within the British Empire and other European colonies.'

Georgia listened silently, saddened by the state of her people around the world.

'Would you believe we were actually turned away from some of the museums and restaurants in New York? Nathan's uncle had to recommend specific venues so we could avoid the embarrassment.'

'They should be the ones who are embarrassed,' Georgia remonstrated.

'Indeed. I'm embarrassed on behalf of my race and their ignorance. I'm pleased to say that I'm not the only one. You have support from many walks of life,' said Daniel, disgusted at what he was hearing. How many times had he called out the prejudice that some of his parishioners could not hide? He'd even had to admonish some of his family for their prejudiced views. It was shameful and tiresome.

'It's truly disturbing. However, it's not for you to carry that burden, Daniel. You've always been an active ally and supporter of radical justice and equality,' Nathan reassured him.

'We've had to be incredibly resilient as a people in general. In New York, we've built our own churches, corporations, libraries, theatres, schools ... you name it. That's why we must continue to support the choirs and lecturers who travel here to raise money for the development of the race,' Celia declared proudly.

'Most of those choirs are styled after the phenomenal Fisk Jubilee Singers. Many organisations and businesses have been forced into integrating their employment practices, services, and premises as a result of our lobbying and protesting,' Nathan explained.

'Good,' said Georgia with satisfaction.

Celia smirked. 'I brought some Black-owned newspapers for you to read.'

'Oh, goody,' Georgia practically squealed. Laughter filled the room. Georgia was usually so guarded and sardonic in nature—Celia wondered if the abandoned baby had softened her sharp edges or if it was a certain handsome, blue-eyed gentleman.

'Remember the concert we attended last year?'

'The coloured American choir?' Georgia confirmed.

'Yes. We attended another of their concerts in New York. It was fabulous. We must attend another one here when the next choir visits. They've been very popular. We'll have to buy our tickets the minute they're advertised,' said Celia.

Celia smiled serenely and gave Georgia an odd look. 'One night, we met a friend for dinner in Harlem. She gave me something for you.' Celia took out a letter from her silver-beaded handbag and handed it to a puzzled Georgia.

Unshed tears shone in Georgia's eyes when she recognised the writing on the front of the envelope. Overcome with emotion, she blew Celia a grateful kiss—it was a letter from her precious sister, Amelia. 'Thank you, but how?' Georgia whispered hoarsely.

Daniel reached out to squeeze her hand comfortingly.

Celia exchanged looks with Nathan. *How wonderful if those two could come together,* she thought gleefully.

Nathan caught her eye again. Celia had known Nathan long enough to recognise that look. It was a silent warning for her not to interfere or get any ideas. She sighed inwardly. *Men—they were no fun when it came to romance.*

She turned back to Georgia. 'I don't want to spoil the letter. Amelia explains everything.'

'Thanks for a lovely day. Lunch was delicious.' Georgia smiled up at Daniel, who had joined her at the parlour window to wave goodbye to Celia and Nathan as their hansom cab pulled away.

She let go of the curtains, which were now drawn across the wooden shutters to keep out the chilly spring evening. Georgia shivered.

'You're very much welcome. It was my pleasure.'
Daniel returned her smile.

'Are you cold?' He stared down at her with his sharp,
navy-blue eyes.

'Not really. There is a bit of a draft. Let's move back to
the seating area,' Georgia said shyly.

She gasped as Daniel gently stroked her bottom lip
with his thumb. The shock of the gesture and the erotic
feel of his surprisingly soft thumb rendered her speechless.

'I've always thought your lips to be quite
tantalising ... and luscious.'

Georgia remained still as Daniel continued to stroke
her lips. They gazed at each other, transfixed. He moved
towards her as if in slow motion and pressed his firm
mouth to her lips. Her mouth opened of its own accord,
as if without her permission. She raised a hand and placed
it behind his strong neck, stroking the soft hairs layered
at the back of it, revelling in the light scent of his soap
and aftershave, a mix of lemon and spice.

Their tongues met and danced around each other,
playing tag and it. Daniel used both hands to explore her
shapely, petite figure. The feel of his hands and mouth
was simply delightful, and her insides were like liquid.
She sighed and pressed herself against his tall, muscular
body, her full breasts aligned with his wide chest. He

moaned his approval, and they continued their decadent tongue play.

They couldn't get enough of each other, and their tongues moved on to play hide and seek. Daniel pulled away slightly and nibbled at her bottom lip. Georgia felt helpless. She was so soft and pliable in his capable hands. She leaned back slightly and reluctantly put some distance between them.

'I'm sorry'—Daniel stared down at her, smiling widely, not looking sorry at all—'I couldn't resist.'

'I ...' Georgia tried and failed to respond. She felt like one of those silly women in one of those popular penny novels Celia loved to read. Her romantic experiences with previous suitors had been nothing like this.

Georgia turned unsteadily and walked to one of the sofas, trying hard not to tremble. Daniel strode over like a big cat and sat down beside her. He took her hands in his and stroked her knuckles idly.

'Have you thought about my proposal?'

'That's not fair,' Georgia protested. 'I'm a mess right now. I can't think straight.'

Daniel put his head back and laughed joyously.

'It's not funny.' Georgia struggled to remain serious at his mirth. He looked so different when he laughed, his strong, white, teeth. She touched her lips subconsciously and sighed. 'You don't look or act like a curate,' Georgia replied grudgingly.

'I don't feel like your typical curate most of the time,' Daniel confessed. 'I'm playing a role that allows me to praise God and serve him through the community the best way I know how. It's a calling of sorts, but it doesn't change the fact that I'm still a red-blooded male, as they say. You forget my past reputation, my dearest Georgia.'

'Who could forget! And I'm not *your* Georgia,' she said haughtily.

Their eyes met, and they burst out laughing.

'I'm not the marrying type. Anyway, what would your family say? I'm not exactly the type of suitor they would have imagined for you.'

'Why?'

'Oh, Daniel, must you act so obtuse? I'm not white enough for them. I might be the offspring of a member of the gentry, but you know I still don't quite fit in because of my mother's race.'

Daniel frowned and put his hands earnestly together. 'I don't care what my family think, Georgia. I'm my own man. I hardly see them.'

Georgia opened her mouth to speak, but Daniel held up his hand. 'And as for your little revelation about your innocence, I don't care about that either. I'm not exactly in a moral position to judge,' he said nonchalantly.

Georgia cleared her throat, her cheeks flushed, embarrassed at his outburst regarding her lack of virginity. She bowed her head. 'I shouldn't have blurted it out like that.'

'Is he someone I have to be concerned about?' Daniel asked stiffly.

'No. He is deceased. He was in the Navy. He died in an accident,' said Georgia sadly.

'Oh ... I'm sorry. I shouldn't have pried. May his soul rest in eternal peace.'

'Thank you. And, no, that's perfectly all right. You had a right to know that I would not be coming to the marriage bed innocent. However, I could have announced it in a more refined manner.'

'Does that mean you accept my proposal?'

Georgia nodded hesitantly.

Daniel brought one of her hands to his lips. 'Thank you. I feel blessed.'

Tears came to Georgia's eyes. 'I cannot allow little Nicholas to be looked after by strangers or looked down upon by polite society. I'm not the maternal type, but I've grown to love him and cannot bear to part with him. Are you really prepared to go through with an arranged marriage?'

'Not really. I'm not the marrying type either, and you're not the only one getting used to the idea. We both have good reasons: you need a father for the little one, and I need my uncle's inheritance to set up more charitable projects.'

Daniel lifted Georgia's chin. 'I feel we've become good friends. We have lots in common. There's no denying there's a strong attraction between us—don't you think that's a good start?'

'I hope so,' whispered Georgia.

CHAPTER SIX

'Congratulations on your engagement!' Celia announced with joy and happiness for her best friend in the world. She fluttered her lashes so as to prevent unshed tears from spilling onto her high cheekbones.

'Thank you,' said Georgia and Daniel simultaneously.

'Oh, see? They already have one mind,' tittered Jenny, Georgia's housekeeper and Celia's good friend. She clapped her pale, freckled hands excitedly.

Their guests laughed, all except Marshal Harcourt, whose broad, handsome features wore a concerned look.

'I must say, Daniel, I'm surprised you would make such a hasty decision in the circumstances.'

Daniel sighed. Marshal did not believe in the races mixing, though he had become one of Daniel's closest religious confidantes.

Georgia studied Marshal seriously, irritated at the turn in tone. She and Daniel had gathered some of their friends from the literary society to join them for a light evening meal and to announce their engagement. The meal had been prepared by Celia and Jenny, a delicious mix of West Indian, Southern American and British dishes, showcasing Celia's heritage.

They had moved into Georgia's large but cosy parlour for coffee and dessert. It was also an opportunity to discuss the last book they had read and which literary choice to read next. For once, the main members of the literary society were all in attendance: Nathan, Celia, Jenny, Georgia's clerk, Tom, and a special guest, Marshal Harcourt. Marshal was a renowned activist, theology student and speaker for the Temperance Movement and colonial matters having an impact on the Black race in Africa and the Diaspora.

Marshal was a great speaker and intellect. He did not drink, of course, so he had chosen to raise his glass filled with sweet homemade lemonade. After his outburst, the jovial, relaxed atmosphere became slightly tense whilst the group waited for the newly engaged couple to respond to the outspoken activist.

Daniel had chosen to stay silent once he realised that Georgia was gearing up to speak. He had got used to the intense stare that was so often directed at him when they had first got to know each other and tended to rub each other the wrong way.

'You realise I'm half white? It's not exactly out of the ordinary in London,' Georgia growled.

'And what if you wish to travel to America, as has been discussed?' Marshal raised a thick black eyebrow. 'You know they will make your life a living hell in certain parts. Even in New York, you will meet with hostility from both sides, as have many mixed couples of different persuasions.'

Daniel placed a reassuring hand on Marshal's arm. 'My friend, I think it is best that we cross that bridge when we come to it. In the meantime, we'll deal with the bigots in England one case at a time.'

Georgia smiled lightly at Daniel whilst warning Marshal to dare to take the subject any further with her fiery hazel-grey eyes. She wondered if this was cause for concern for their well-being or some level of sour grapes talking. At one time, long before she had known Daniel as a friend of Nathan's, Marshal had expressed an interest in her. Still in mourning for her deceased beau, she had not been interested. Although there was no denying that he was attractive and striking with his broad build, smooth, perfect, ebony-toned complexion, strong, noble features, and large almond-shaped eyes, he reminded her of an ancient Kemetic pharaoh, with his strong, Nubian features. His soft, wool-like hair was cut short on his square-jawed head.

Georgia had always felt that his general temperament was a little too serious for her. He had some strange ideas about the submissiveness of women, which were too extreme for her nature. She was happy for her partner to lead, but not in an autocratic manner—she would always want a say in her own future. She suspected that even he realised she was a tad too headstrong and independent for him. Circumstances had made her so.

Despite being quite opinionated on many subjects, Marshal could not be accused of being insensitive to the change in atmosphere and the wary look in Georgia's eyes. 'Pray tell, I suspect I need to tread lightly here. Despite my reservations, I genuinely wish you both well. You've both been incredibly supportive of my endeavours, and I'm truly grateful to call you my friends. Please forgive me my indiscretion.'

'Well, Marshal, you're not known for your discretion. What you see is what you get, I'll give you that,' said Daniel with an amused look on his face. He also suspected there was more to the outburst than a concern for how society would react to their relationship.

The atmosphere in the room visibly lightened as the guests—including Marshal—chuckled at Daniel's honest observation of his friend.

'Well, I, for one, am chuffed about your news. It's a relief to know Miss Georgia will be looked after.' Tom,

Georgia's loyal clerk, held up his hand in the face of Georgia's horrified protests, his pale-grey eyes earnest.

'No, Miss Georgia. It's been quite worrying leaving you here each evening unprotected, especially now that both Miss Celia and Miss Amelia have moved on to greener pastures. It's been even more worrying since you've brought the little baby on board. Everyone deserves a family—I wouldn't be without my Holly and the two little ones.'

Georgia caught Daniel's warning eye and sighed inwardly, then beamed gratefully at Daniel as he swiftly changed the subject. 'So, where are you lecturing this month, Marshal?' asked Daniel, clearing his throat and trying not to blush at Georgia's captivating smile.

Marshal, always observant of human peccadilloes, smiled with amusement at seeing his cool and collected friend affected by a woman's pearly whites for once in his life.

Marshal had been born in Antigua. He had stowed away as a young boy and ended up in America. The son of a schoolteacher, he had attended a chapel school back home. Once in New York, he found it hard to stomach the treatment of Black people in the North. He had worked for a Black newspaper for a while, but heard from friends that England, although challenging, did not have systemic racial segregation. There was a colour bar instigated in some high and low places, but it was not as harsh as in America or in the range of British colonies he could have chosen from. The colour bar occasionally occurred in pubs, workplaces, shops, boarding houses, the shipping industry and other commercial enterprises. People of colour also had a tough time entering and maintaining a political stance, although there had been some rare success stories. It was both systemic and economic, depending on your class and financial status. Regardless of whether you were considered one of the Black elite or a well-connected activist, you were still, to a certain extent, expected to know your place and toe the line in many circumstances.

Marshal had, on a number of occasions, complained to Daniel that he had not been allowed to join one of the many gentlemen's clubs dotted throughout London so he could lobby for his many causes. It was a world of white, upper-class men and some women, a small set of elites and fashionable ranks who socialised in the clubs of the West End in Pall Mall and Piccadilly.

Daniel had left that world behind for the most part and had no real desire to be a part of anything that wouldn't allow many of his friends and acquaintances of colour or whites of the lower-class to join. He was reluctantly persuaded by Nathan and Marshal to network to raise money and create influence for their political, charitable and social causes on their behalf.

Nathan interjected (he had been rather quiet for most of the evening): 'Yes, Marshal—tell us what your plans are. I'm eager to attend another of your lectures. I need to hear how the race has been enduring in America since Celia and I have returned from our wonderful honeymoon.'

Marshal leant forward. 'I'm lecturing in Croydon next Thursday evening about the lynchings in America. It's a disgrace that post-slavery and all this time after reconstruction, we cannot escape these atrocities.'

The group murmured in agreement and disgust.

'I'm also in Bristol later on in the month to lecture about higher amount of traffic to West Africa on behalf of the Temperance Society. Over the next few months, I'll be teaching on various subjects in Plymouth, Cardiff, Liverpool and even Edinburgh. It's pleasing to note that although in the minority, the audience consists of a good many in British society who are not happy with the way coloured people are treated either here or in the Diaspora and ex-colonies,' announced Marshal proudly.

'Celia has been helping me with the publicity side of things, for which I am eternally grateful.'

Celia smiled graciously. 'My pleasure. How do you manage your studies with all these engagements?'

'I have to pay for my Theology course. As you know, I was unable to apply for a scholarship on time as I'd spent so much time in America.'

'Which organisations do you lecture for?' Tom asked, curious to hear more about their well-travelled, special guest.

'Mainly the Christian Evidence Society and the Temperance Society. My political and social activism regarding race ties in nicely. I feel obligated to lead people and society back to godly endeavours. A spiritual way of life is essential to our enlightenment.' He looked around the group, clearly pleased to see some nodding heads in agreement.

'So many of our race have been led astray by drink and a lack of control in terms of their social behaviours, mostly due to poverty as well as the mental and spiritual burden of our positions in society. Those of us in privileged positions must do all we can to reach back and pull our fellow brothers and sisters up by their bootstraps if necessary.'

'Hear, Hear,' said Daniel enthusiastically.

Jenny and Tom turned to Daniel in astonishment. Jenny's honey-blonde top bun almost toppled as she swivelled in her position across the room.

'Yes, I know I'm not of the race, but in my vocation, I genuinely see all races as my fellow men, brothers and sisters in Christ. How else could I feel in view of my upcoming nuptials to my beautiful, soon-to-be wife? Although I don't think any of us are anywhere near giving up on a soothing glass of wine or spirits any time soon, from the looks of this gathering.'

'I agree you are a friend and brother in Christ.' Marshal sprang forward to shake Daniel's hand vigorously, to the amusement of the group.

'And on that notable confession, referring to your own admirable temperance, may I help myself to a jug of your lemonade? I confess I, myself, am battling an annoyingly sweet tooth.'

'So, what do you think of our next book choice?' asked Daniel.

'Gerald Massey's writing is interesting, to say the least,' Georgia answered thoughtfully. 'Mind you, I'm going to miss reading Olaudah's innocent intriguing story about life on the treacherous seas. There's an endearing innocence about him.'

Their guests had discreetly left them to their own devices a little earlier. Jenny had retired to her room after she had supervised the housemaid's tidying of the basement kitchen in the servants' quarters. Baby Nicholas had settled in with Nanny Laurel in the nursery quarters. It was not that Georgia was so bothered about polite society's segregation of the nursery and servants' quarters—she regularly sat in the room next to the kitchen downstairs to plan the week's meals or have a quick chat, much to the new housemaid's horror—she had just never quite got used to being mistress of her domain. She had also not quite changed the habits she'd acquired while younger, as a sociable child growing up in a large household and then at boarding school. Airs and graces were just not her thing. The communal living style of her noble African ancestors would have been perfect for her.

'Does Massey really believe the origin of religion, in particular, is in Africa?'

'Yes, he does, and I'd love to attend one of his lectures to pick his brain. He's in good company with Herodotus, Diodorus, Plato and other Greek scholars,' said Daniel. They were planning to read two of Massey's works, *A Book of the Beginnings* and *The Natural Genesis*.

'Indeed, but how, pray, does this sit with your vocation as a curate?'

Daniel walked over to sit beside her on the plush settee and placed a long arm across the back of it. 'Anything that forces me to question my beliefs is welcome. Enlightenment has always been my spiritual goal. It won't take away from my belief in the greatest power there is, the Most High God. I will say this: there is no doubt, based on the evidence, experiences and research of so many scholars, that African and human civilisation started in the Nile Valley areas.'

Georgia nodded her head enthusiastically. 'Oh, I have to agree. The evidence is undeniable, and, of course, many credible scholars and historians do agree. But the dissenters will always try to dehumanise people of African descent and make us seem primitive with their pseudo-science.

'And what's wrong with being primitive? It simply means the first or original, if we put it into context. It's so frustrating to have our image so disgracefully distorted to uphold the legacy of slavery and colonialism,' huffed Georgia.

'I've learnt so much from Nathan and his research collection. His library is like an Aladdin's cave of African and human history, especially his information on Kush or the Nubian civilisation, as some like to call it.' Daniel shifted closer to Georgia.

Nathan, Celia's husband, was an aspiring politician and an amateur scholar and historian. He came from a wealthy merchant family based in Sierra Leone. Growing up, he had been taught by a renowned African scholar before being sent to England to boarding school. After leaving school, he spent many years in the Navy as a petty officer and also funded his own travels across the African continent and to other places around the globe. During his global travels, he collected as much information as he could, including papers, books, pamphlets, and newspapers to do with Africa, the Diaspora and the world, to add to the precious books and scripts his tutor and family had secured for him. Lately, since he'd settled back in England, some historians travelled increasingly far and wide to view his collection.

'Who would believe there are more pyramids in Sudan than in the area they call modern Egypt today? It's all so fascinating.' Georgia leaned into the crook of Daniel's arm and smiled up at him.

'Almost as fascinating as you.' Daniel smiled and leaned into a searing kiss from his betrothed.

'I wish we'd had a quick wedding,' whispered Georgia, pulling reluctantly away.

'Steady on. You'll have to be patient. You can't have your wicked way with me just yet.' Georgia patted him lightly on his muscular arm.

'Ouch,' responded Daniel in mock pain.

'Oh, don't be dramatic. I barely touched you.' Georgia laughed. Daniel laughed and kissed her on her forehead. They relaxed in each other's arms for a moment.

'Daniel? What is it like to be a philanderer?'

Daniel regarded her with a surprised expression on his face. He rubbed his jaw, looking uncomfortable. 'Do you really want to know?'

'I wouldn't have asked if I didn't.'

Daniel smiled ruefully. That was what he loved about Georgia. Her outspokenness meant she wasn't afraid to hear the truth, no matter the situation. They were kindred spirits, similar in that sense. He blinked, having caught himself using the word love. Had he been falling for her all this time? He didn't know what true love was, but he did know he felt alive and vibrant in her presence, as if a dim gas light had been turned up in his heart, brightening his whole being while in her presence.

Georgia was constantly in his thoughts. She made him laugh and brought out his protective instincts. He longed for the day he would make sweet love to her in their marriage bed and anywhere else she wished to express their attraction. Georgia emanated strength, sensuality and femininity. There was so much more under the surface to explore. *Was that love?* Curate or not, he had a healthy appetite for lovemaking, and he needed a wife who would match his needs in a healthy, loving, respectful marriage. He sensed he had met his match in Georgia.

Daniel smiled at Georgia. She was wiggling her eyebrows, waiting for him to reveal his past in all its shameful glory. 'I fear you will look at me differently if I reveal too much.'

Georgia rolled her eyes. 'My dear, the rumour mill has surpassed anything you could possibly tell me." Georgia grimaced in mock disapproval. "I suspect your version is much tamer.'

Daniel chuckled. Still unsure where to start, he hesitated.

Georgia decided to help him along: 'Did you have a paramour, a mistress?'

'Yes, I did.'

'Who was she?'

Daniel raised an eyebrow. 'I was sworn to secrecy, and I wouldn't break that promise, even for you. I'm ashamed to admit that she was a married woman.'

'Hmm … fair enough,' Georgia replied grudgingly with a look that implied she approved of his discretion despite her curiosity.

'Truth be told, I enjoyed my time as a shameless rake. It was .. . enlightening in terms of the peccadilloes of various grown women. Am I proud of it? No. Did I eventually become exasperated and lose a little of my soul with the drama of each affair and all the drinking and carousing at gentlemen's clubs that went with it? Yes. It wasn't the most uplifting lifestyle. I couldn't carry on living in such a disruptive and destructive manner. Eventually, I became morose and unhappy. Hence, my spiritual epiphany. I don't completely regret it … I know what I'm not missing as a curate who has to exercise a degree of self-control. It has allowed me to focus on nurturing my relationship with God.'

He pulled back from Georgia slightly. 'I'd like to think it makes me somewhat less judgmental than your average man of the cloth when it comes to human falls from grace and temptations of the flesh.'

Georgia listened intently, leaning into the light stroke of his fingers on the soft skin at the back of her neck. 'I admire you, Daniel. It couldn't have been easy to leave that lifestyle behind.'

Daniel looked down at Georgia in pleasant surprise. He felt a warm heat of pride rise up through his chest at the compliment. No one in his family had ever expressed their pride in his change of life and purpose. And certainly none of his former crowd, who had hung on to his every word in clubland and his coattails in the various boudoirs of disrepute. It felt exhilarating to have someone whose opinion he cared about validate the effort it had taken to turn his future around.

In light of the fact that she was not ashamed when she'd made her own confession regarding her lack of innocence, he found her transparency refreshing, and he respected her need to be honest with him. Although he had felt a sharp stab of jealousy at the poor deceased soul who had taken her innocence. Georgia had a healthy attitude when it came to the needs of a marriage and their duties as husband and wife. Their interactions gave him a glance into their future as husband and wife.

Although Georgia did not attend church every Sunday, she had always been involved in various charitable causes, locally and globally. Most importantly, she had a strong faith, and they were a good match both socially and culturally. With his support, they would work through the societal challenges that came with Georgia being Anglo-African and him being white, giving thanks that they had similar backgrounds, shared friends and many interests in common. He prayed that God would help him protect her and baby Nicholas and provide for their needs—physically, mentally and spiritually.

'Thank you for the acknowledgement. I don't think you know how much it means to be validated by you.' He kissed her tenderly on her full, eager lips.'

'I think we're going to have an interesting marriage, Daniel,' murmured Georgia.

'Hmm,' Daniel hummed in agreement as he worked more kisses down the side of her neck.

CHAPTER SEVEN

'I want him back,' Betsy O'Sullivan announced, lifting her plump chin defiantly.

Georgia stared at Betsy as if she had seen an apparition. 'What on Earth?' She shook her head as if to clear it. 'I thought—'

'I know what you thought.' Betsy smiled wryly. 'I faked my death so you would stop looking for me.'

'Wait—let me lock up the shop. Let's go into the office.' Georgia couldn't bear to take Betsy upstairs into her apartments. She didn't want her anywhere near baby Nicholas. Wishing her hands would stop shaking, she drew down the bookshop blinds, turned the 'Back Soon' sign to face the street and locked the door.

Georgia sat across from Betsy in her small, neat, back office. She looked up at the ledgers on the high shelf behind Betsy for a moment to try to gather her thoughts. Slits of sunlight accentuated microscopic dust particles in the atmosphere and on the ledgers. Had she not dusted those only yesterday? Her brain felt foggy—the situation was much too surreal.

Betsy stared at her silently, a defiant expression on her round features. Georgia knew she needed to act cautiously. It would not do to lose her temper, not when there was the possibility of losing something much more precious. Nicholas had become an integral part of her life. She had no intention of giving him up without a fight, but judging from Betsy's demeanour, she knew she had to tread carefully. Judging by her appearance, playing dead had benefitted her healthy, golden skin, indicating she had been somewhere with a lot of sun lately. Her toned skin looked healthy; she'd put on weight, and she wore good-quality clothing.

'What type of mother abandons her child and fakes her death?' Georgia could have kicked herself. That wasn't how she had intended the question to be framed. Oh, why did she have to be such a plain speaker? How she wished Celia could be there to mediate. She had the negotiation skills and temperament of a diplomat. At the same time, she was relieved that Daniel wasn't present. As much as she would have appreciated his support, he would have made mincemeat of this little madam.

'I've always appreciated your honesty'—Betsy smiled knowingly—'but I was desperate. I met an older gentleman who offered to marry me and take care of me.

'But that would have been perfect for baby Nicholas.'

'Baby Nicholas, is it now?' Betsy said scathingly, a sneer on her round face. 'Didn't take you long to endear yourself to the little nuisance.'

'If he's a nuisance, I take it you don't want him back, so why are you here?' Georgia held her hands together as serenely as possible, daring herself not to throw the paperweight on the desk at Betsy. How she could be so heartless and brazen was beyond her understanding.

'Me 'usband—I mean, my husband'—she held out her left hand to show off a rather ostentatious wedding band—'didn't want another man's child.'

Georgia raised a well-shaped eyebrow. Betsy kept swinging between London Cockney and a more pronounced way of speaking. Had she had elocution lessons?

'Anyway, it turns out he most likely can't 'ave children after a short illness.' Betsy patted the back of her black curly bun and cleared her throat self-consciously.

'Well, you can't have him. I've already spoken to the relevant authorities about adoption.'

'He's my child!'

'It's a pity you didn't realise that before you abandoned him in the arms of the local curate.' Georgia regarded Betsy disdainfully.

'He said he'll divorce me if I can't get the child back. I'm not going back to charring and cleaning other people's dirty fireplaces and potties on my hands and knees. I hate that life. I really will kill myself if I have to go back to that.'

Georgia continued to regard her adversary thoughtfully. 'What type of person is your husband to threaten divorce? I know it most likely wasn't a love match, but he must have some redeeming qualities other than wealth.'

'Of course not. I married him for his wealth; he married me for my youth.' Betsy looked at Georgia incredulously, as if she had seen an elephant walk out of her mouth.

She held out her left hand again and waggled her chubby fingers as if to solidify her married status. 'I'm Mrs Rawlings now. My Howard is a canny magistrate, by the way. We live in Croydon. He says you 'ave no legal recourse as I'm alive and married and you're unmarried.' Betsy sniffed self-righteously.

'Who was Nicholas's father?' Betsy's eyes widened at the change of subject and bold questioning. She had always insisted that Nicholas's father never knew she was pregnant, but after this debacle, Georgia could no longer trust that she was telling the truth.

Betsy sighed. 'He was a seaman from the West Indies who emigrated to Canada with his wife. He conveniently didn't care to tell me about her until I'd told him I was with child. I swore then that I would never be in a relationship for love. It's a fool's paradise.'

Georgia found it hard to disagree in the circumstances. She was having a hard time coming to terms with her own feelings about marriage ever since she had become engaged.

As if reading her mind, Betsy eyed the glistening engagement ring on Georgia's left hand.

'When's the happy day?'

'Soon,' Georgia answered vaguely. The last thing she wanted was to discuss her upcoming nuptials.

'Who's the lucky groom?'

Georgia sighed. 'Mr Henderson.'

'The curate?' Betsy's bright brown eyes widened as Georgia nodded in response. 'Well, well.'

'Yes. Well.' Georgia shifted in her seat, feeling awkward discussing her private affairs with this recreant. 'I'll need to discuss this turn of events with him.'

'Well, don't take your time. Me and Howard—I mean, Howard and I—won't be in London for too much longer. We're staying at a lovely little hotel in Kensington. We'll be in touch. Very soon.'

'Very well. I'll see you out.' Georgia stood, relieved to see the back of Betsy....for now.

Later that evening, Georgia swept into Daniel's large study lined with tall bookshelves, her long skirts swishing against the mahogany door as she entered. She had kept the bookshop closed for the day and rushed over to the vestry early to inform him of the latest events in the baby Nicholas saga.

After his initial shock, he suggested that he would arrange to meet with a solicitor friend who attended one of his former gentlemen's clubs. Other than to promote various charitable causes, he had stopped attending when he realised it would be a conflict of interest with his religious vocation. In addition, some of the clubs rarely accepted people of colour or other cultural backgrounds into their confines. It felt wrong to continue to contribute to such a system. He'd had some friends who'd disagreed. In the main, they'd become mere acquaintances.

Georgia had agreed to meet him at his townhouse to discuss the solicitor's feedback, but she stopped short when she noted that Daniel had company. *Female* company.

He rushed over to Georgia as the woman sitting at his desk rose to her feet. Georgia discreetly noted that she was tall and voluptuous with wavy, vibrant auburn hair under an elaborately decorated hat. Her features were too strong to be considered beautiful in Victorian terms, but she was incredibly striking.

Daniel kissed her hand affectionately and drew her over to meet his guest. Georgia caught the displeased narrowing of the attractive woman's pale-grey eyes. Did she detect a mist of venom or had she imagined it?

'Georgia, meet an old family friend of mine: Lady Grace Willoughby.'

Georgia nodded her head politely. 'Good evening. How nice to meet you.' Georgia knew, without a shadow of a doubt, that Lady Willoughby didn't believe a word of her glib lie. They eyed each other knowingly.

'Good evening. I hear congratulations are in order.'

Daniel jumped in. 'I was telling Grace about our upcoming nuptials.'

Lady Willoughby sniffed and pulled on her leather gloves. 'It seems rather rushed, but who am I to stand in the way of true love?' She regarded Georgia with sharp, knowing eyes. Georgia blushed in spite of herself.

'Anyway, it was rather rude of me to visit unannounced, Daniel. It won't happen again, but I couldn't resist popping in and surprising you. I wanted you to know that I was visiting London.

'Good day to you. Maybe I'll see you at the wedding. In the meantime, we must meet for dinner, Daniel.'

Georgia smiled tightly when she noted that the invite to dinner had not included her.

'I'll see you out.' Daniel escorted her out.

Once they had left the room, Georgia drew off her leather gloves crossly and slammed them down onto Daniel's unsuspecting desk. She did not miss the angry whispering outside the door—they were obviously having a heated discussion.

Georgia turned as Daniel re-entered the study a short while later.

'You look lovely, Georgia.'

'Don't you lovely me.' Georgia sniffed. 'How dare you, introduce me to one of your … paramours? Lady, my foot.'

She sensed Daniel was trying not to laugh. 'It's not funny, Daniel.'

'Sorry, no, it's not funny. I was quite angry about her visit. But, as usual, your loose tongue has amused me. *Ex*-paramour, by the way.'

'Ooh, I say,' Georgia said sarcastically, rolling her eyes heavenward.

Daniel took both of Georgia's hands and pulled her gently towards him. She briefly took in his dashing image in his well-cut, patterned-grey waistcoat, white shirt with a high collar and black-and-silver cufflinks. His waistcoat perfectly showcased his long, well-toned arms. No wonder Lady Willoughby was still enraptured by him.

'As you heard, I didn't invite her here. You know I would never do that, and she certainly will not be invited to the wedding. Rather presumptuous of her.' He looked straight into Georgia's eyes. 'Do you believe me?'

Georgia sighed grudgingly. 'Yes.'

Daniel looked relieved. He pecked her on her soft, luscious lips. Georgia responded briefly, then pulled back.

'Let's sit down by the fire.' Daniel rang the servants' bell.

His housekeeper, Mrs Bennett, seemed to appear from nowhere. 'Good morning. I take it you're ready for refreshments, Mr Henderson—coffee or tea?'

Daniel looked across at Georgia.

'Good evening, coffee please, Mrs Bennett,' Georgia asked, giving the plump woman a friendly smile.

'I'll have what my fiancée's having.'

'Of course, Sir. Won't be long.' Mrs Bennet discreetly left the room.

Georgia looked at Daniel expectantly.

'What should we discuss first: baby Nicholas or Lady Grace?' Daniel enquired.

Georgia took a deep breath. 'Baby Nicholas, of course.'

Daniel leaned forward. 'I'm afraid it's bad news.'

Georgia tensed. Her stomach dropped like a grounded ship's anchor.

Daniel pressed his hands together. 'We don't have a leg to stand on, not with Betsy being alive and married to a respected magistrate. I can't believe she managed to pull off such a farce.'

'The private investigator needs to return your money, but what can I say? We all fell for the ruse,' Georgia said.

Daniel shook his head ruefully. 'Indeed. He felt very foolish once I enlightened him. He's a decent man and offered to return my fee, but I wouldn't have it. Nobody could have guessed she was capable of such subterfuge.'

'I know I'm being unfair to him, but I feel so frustrated and cheated. Am I selfish to want to keep him from his mother?' She looked at Daniel earnestly.

'Of course not.' He reached his arm over to cup her cheek and turned her face to him. 'You obviously love him. His so-called mother clearly doesn't. She's using him now that she needs him to solidify her new lifestyle at her husband's bequest.'

'What are we going to do?' Georgia asked.

Daniel got up and drew her into a warm, comforting embrace. 'I have no idea.'

Georgia sent up a silent prayer.

CHAPTER EIGHT

Daniel closed his Bible as the Bible class came to an end. It was mid-week, and he had persuaded Georgia to join his lecture on a passage from the Bible—it was a passage on loss.

It had been a devastating week for both of them. They had become distant as they both dealt with the hurt of having to return baby Nicholas to his recreant mother. Georgia threw herself into growing the bookshop, while Daniel threw himself into his parish duties.

They had planned to eat a light supper at a local restaurant after Bible class. In the meantime, Daniel needed to mingle with the small congregation whilst they said their goodbyes and asked questions. Georgia offered to take some of the Bibles into the vestry and wait for him there. She wasn't in the mood to mingle.

In London, most parishes had the clergymen supported by curates, lecturers and readers. As a curate and lecturer, Daniel assisted the clergy across two parishes in Bloomsbury and Soho in various works. He read passages from the scripture and commented on them, both on Sundays and mid-week. He also performed services in other local churches when needed.

Daniel was one in a wide network of clergymen who worked together for the well-being and spiritual welfare of the well-to-do and poorer urban populations. Most curates were not paid much, but they could make a living and build a reputation for themselves by speaking on passages from the Scriptures two to three times a week. This was even more likely if the lectureship was funded by parishioners or benefaction organisations. Daniel was fortunate not to rely on benefactors, as he benefited from a generous trust fund set up by his grandparents for him and his siblings. He also had various investments and business interests.

His uncle's inheritance would be used to set up a soup kitchen for struggling parishioners, many of whom lived in Argyle Square. In addition, he hoped he would be able to open a boarding house for Black and Indian sailors at some point.

He smiled as he entered the back room, where Georgia was sitting. He'd missed her and was looking forward to spending time with her during their meal. Maybe they would start to heal from the devastating blow of losing baby Nicholas.

Daniel was moody as he smoked his pipe in his parlour. He stared at the glistening engagement ring lying on the small, round coffee table beside him. It was no longer on Georgia's left hand, and she was no longer his betrothed. He wondered how he had ended up wifeless and childless within a few days.

Earlier that evening ...

'Your skin is amazingly soft—it's like silk,' Daniel mused, examining Georgia reverently with his hands and eyes. Georgia was a vision in a pale blue corset, which emphasised her shapely figure, along with a white petticoat and pantaloons. She held out one shapely leg as they sat on the edge of Daniel's bed, and Daniel cupped her heel. He had just pulled off one of her lace-topped stockings, pushed her back onto the bed and ran his hand along the soft skin of her thighs. They released mutual sighs of pleasure as he kissed her décolletage and delicious, slender neck.

He shivered as her hands ran down his wide shoulders and across his broad back. He had somehow lost his shirt and waistcoat earlier. He wore a pair of trousers, waistband undone and hanging loosely at his hips. How they had come to be in the dimly lit boudoir area of his large apartments was a distant memory. He barely remembered getting heated in the parlour and carrying her up the stairs at her request.

Mercifully, the female staff lived out. He had no need for a valet or butler other than on special occasions, which didn't happen often since he'd become a curate. In theory, this little soiree was totally unorthodox behaviour for anyone in polite society, let alone a curate. But knowing what polite society was truly like and knowing himself well, the practice was not so unorthodox—he would only allow intimacies with Georgia to go so far.

He gasped when Georgia pulled his head up, urging him to move higher. He covered her face with gentle kisses and continued to stroke her all over her body.

'Hmm ... Daniel,' Georgia whispered.

'Your freckles are the most adorable thing.' He kissed her across the bridge of her small, rounded nose. Heated pressure built inside him as she ran her tongue up the curve of his strong neck, her body fitting perfectly into the comfort of his embrace.

They kissed and stroked each other. Her mouth opened to allow his tongue deeper entry, and she released a low moan as the heated love play grew more and more intense with each long, drawn-out kiss.

Her hands roamed his lithe, toned body, just as keen to fulfil her needs. They moved against each other, her legs wrapped around him, the evidence of his growing arousal obvious.

'We need to be careful.' Daniel fought his natural urges, exercising caution.

Georgia sighed and pushed him back slightly, the heat in her hazel-grey eyes starting to dim as the realisation of his abrupt interruption set in.

He regretted not being able to love her fully, but he couldn't allow his carnal instincts to take over completely. They'd be married soon, and he needed to be patient. He suspected that once they had consummated their marriage, he was at risk of turning into a lovesick fool. He smiled inwardly at the thought. Thankfully, he had fallen deeply for the stunning woman, who had agreed to marry him to protect Baby Nicholas. He had every hope that their relationship would become a love match.

'Daniel?' Georgia pulled away completely. She sat up in the bed.

'What is it?' Daniel looked up at her. He was lying on his side, leaning on his elbow.

'I can't marry you,' Georgia said, a sad look on her face.

'What on earth?' Daniel shot up.

Georgia placed a finger on his mouth, which was slightly open, ready to protest. He played between biting it in frustration or sucking it gently. *What was wrong with the female species? Why on earth were some of them so contrary?*

'I ... I wanted to marry you for the baby's sake. Now that he's gone, I don't think I can go through with it.'

'But what about what we've shared? Doesn't it mean anything to you?'

Georgia breathed in deeply, avoiding the hurt apparent in Daniel's deep-blue eyes, as well as his voice.

'We got a bit carried away. I've enjoyed it, but I can't base a marriage on lust.'

'Lust? Oh, I'm sorry—I thought genuine feelings were involved, but I was obviously wrong.' He twisted away from her and sat on the edge of the bed, his head in his hands.

'I like you.'

'Like?' He stiffened and raised his head. Daniel had never been so insulted in all his life. He could not overcome his hurt ego. He felt her hand on his shoulder and fought not to shake it off.

'To be honest, I don't know how I feel. There is an undeniable attraction between us, but how do I define it other than lust? Events have moved very quickly.'

Daniel turned to regard her. 'And what about our agreement regarding my inheritance? You know how important opening the soup kitchen and boarding house is to me.'

'I'm sure you could find someone else to marry—what about Lady Grace?'

'What? No.' Daniel shook his head vigorously.

'I'm sorry, but I have too many doubts.' Georgia kissed him softly.

He watched her, stunned, as she picked up her clothing and went to his dressing room. When Georgia returned, he was still sitting on the edge of his bed, hoping she would change her mind but not knowing the right words to say to help influence her decision.

She placed her engagement ring on his side table and exited the room quietly.

CHAPTER NINE

'Are you sure you've made the right decision?' Celia regarded Georgia with concern in her eyes.

Georgia popped a piece of succulent meat into her mouth. She hadn't eaten much since breakfast—the shop had been busy that day. 'This meal is delicious, Celia,' Georgia said.

'I agree,' Nathan said. His eyes met Celia's.

'Would you both stop giving each other those worrying glances, please? You're not being as discreet as you might think.' Georgia frowned.

Celia and Nathan smiled at Georgia's typical bluntness.

Georgia sighed. 'Part of me feels it was all for nothing, but I obviously value real love, and more than I thought. I couldn't bring myself to marry a man who didn't love me. Not without little Nicholas as the glue.'

'Do you love him?' Nathan asked, his handsome brown face curious.

'Nathan, we've been family friends for a long time, and you are like a brother to me—more than my own brother; however, discussing feelings is talk strictly for Celia and Georgia.' Georgia fixed her gaze firmly on the plate of food. She felt the flush rising up her neck and into her cheeks.

'Hmm.' Nathan smiled at Celia. 'Let me know when she admits to having feelings for her former intended. I'm determined to win our wager.'

'Nathan!' Celia said.

Nathan grinned treacherously.

Georgia almost choked whilst swallowing her wine. 'I knew it! You're both outrageous.'

'Don't be a hypocrite. I distinctly recall Amelia admitting that you'd both taken wagers on how quickly I would change my mind about my feelings towards Nathan.' Celia had been in a dilemma at the time, torn between two loves, Nathan and Edward Langdon.

Placing wagers on the fates of each other's relationships was a habit they had both indulged in since boarding school. Nathan had embraced that tradition once he'd reconnected with Celia and Georgia on his return from New York as a widower with a small child, a sweet little minx named Eloiuse.

Georgia tried to hide her smile, determined to remain stern. They were all guilty of wagering. She had triumphantly won the wager with her sister, as she knew her closest and dearest friend in the world much too well.

Georgia had not seen Daniel for nearly two weeks outside of the charity affairs and her sporadic attendance at church. They were cordial but awkward, to say the least. They'd agreed to continue attending the literary society, but he'd not appeared so far. She was loath to admit that she missed his presence. She longed for his touch, for his kisses—

'How's Marshal?' Celia asked Nathan. Georgia couldn't hide the relief on her face when Celia changed the subject.

'Feeling very sorry for himself,' Nathan confirmed. 'He's left the hospital and is being looked after by one of his "lady friends".'

Celia rolled her eyes.

Nathan chuckled. 'They're fighting over themselves to decide who will nurse him back to health. His landlady isn't happy that he needs the help.'

The Caribbean activist had been followed home by a group of white men after a Temperance lecture. One of them had been an American ex-soldier, now living in Britain. He'd been unhappy about Marshal's stance on the situation of Black people in America who were being gradually forced into segregation, the Jim Crow laws, lynching, and being prevented from voting and practising law. Homes, churches and other Black institutions and property were being attacked and destroyed, especially in the Southern states.

In some areas, Black people had to travel in smoking cars or cattle carriages on trains. In some states, there were vagrancy laws linked to being unemployed, forcing children and adults back into a form of servitude. Some Black children had been forced into signing life long, indentured servitude contracts to work on plantations. It was humiliating, damaging and a worrying setback since the early days of the abolition of slavery after the Civil War and Reconstruction.

An off-duty policeman had also been involved in the attack, which was nothing unusual. Some of the police had a disdain for non-Blacks and whites from poorer classes. They also tended to be disliked by the establishment. Ironically, it was the establishment they were originally set up to protect rather than the general public. It didn't help that they were poorly paid and tended to be recruited from the dubious enclaves of society. Corruption was rife.

'Oh, dear. Send Marshal my best,' Georgia said, bemused by his admirers, who were fighting to heal him and disgusted at the attack. 'I'm relieved he's recovering. We need people like him to continue travelling and sharing knowledge of the race globally.

'Indeed,' Nathan said. 'He is seeking legal representation. Unlike America, if successful as a Black man, he can at least testify against a white man over here.' Nathan shook his head. 'This pathology is complex and dangerous to our race.'

Georgia nodded in agreement.

'It's a bit of a façade, painting Britain in a certain light when it comes to our history. Yet, at the same time, many of the race in the colonies and ex-colonies are being treated with barely any decorum or decency. People need to know the details of the activities the government is carrying out in their name,' Celia said.

'No wonder some Black Americans continue to flee to Canada, the Caribbean, Africa and Europe. As problematic as those areas are politically and economically, they might still be a better option for some, especially those suffering in the South. Amelia told me that many Southerners were part of a great escape to the West of America. That's why she was so excited about emigrating to a Black-founded town. I truly worry about her.' Georgia shook her head thoughtfully.

'Do you understand why Daniel and I insisted on accompanying both of you to the women's suffrage meetings?' Nathan said, frowning.

'Yes. It was terrifying when that horrible man disrupted the meeting with his reprobate crew.' Celia made a face of disgust.

A few months back, Celia and Georgia had attended a small meeting about women's suffrage in a large pharmacy owned by a local married couple. One of the attendees' husband and his friends had thrown bricks through the windows, breaking them, making his feelings clear about the right for women to vote. Both Celia and Georgia had experienced minor cuts and bruises from the glass and the rush as everyone ran through to the safety of the back of the shop. Luckily, no one was seriously hurt, and the men had been run off and confronted by another group of men passing by. The police were fetched, and the men tracked down not too long thereafter, they were now facing charges.

Women generally attended suffrage meetings with some men at town halls to campaign for reforms and increase the number of working-class men who qualified to vote via ownership of property qualifications. It was also not acceptable for women to attend smaller gatherings held at chop houses and public houses frequented by men. The Industrial Revolution provided women with the means to be independent, but they still faced unequal pay and subservient roles, as well as being held back from advancing.

From the mid-nineteenth century, women across Britain became engaged in a struggle to secure voting rights, win the rights to own property and gain access to higher education. Both Celia and Georgia had struggled with the burden of losing their rights to their money and assets, as these would potentially become the property of their husbands if certain restrictive legalities were not put into place. Even worse, the right to make personal decisions about their well-being and way of life could be lost, which could place them and other women in dangerous situations. Many a wife or daughter had ended up in an asylum if they challenged their husbands, fathers, elders, or even male siblings.

'Well, the current rage of tearooms for ladies, where we can meet to discuss women's suffrage, seems to be gaining traction. With a bit of luck, we'll soon be able to secure a local tearoom to arrange our own meetings. I'm determined to support these causes, and a tearoom would be the perfect environment to bring women from different classes and backgrounds together,' Georgia said.

'Hopefully, Celia's idea to extend the bookshop's range to include stationery will boost our income and, in turn, we can continue to support Marshal's and other fundraising efforts for various causes.' Georgia beamed at Celia, who smiled self-consciously. They continued to discuss their business interests over the remainder of their dinner.

Later that evening, Georgia was accosted by Jenny, her housekeeper, as she took off her soft leather gloves in the passageway and placed them on the hallway table. 'Good evening, Georgia. You have a visitor.'

'Good evening, Jenny. Now, who has taken it into their head to visit me at this time of night?' She was still enthused by all the business talk and helping the race both in Africa and the Diaspora at dinner earlier, but she was now feeling quite tired and not in the mood for visitors.

She unpinned her felt green hat carefully in the hallway mirror and placed it on the hall table, next to her gloves.

'A Lady Willoughby?'

Georgia raised her eyebrows with widened eyes and regarded Jenny with confusion. She entered the dimly lit parlour to find said Lady standing by the Japanese-style fireguard positioned regally in front of the fireplace. She was examining the portrait of Georgia's parents on the wall.

Lady Willoughby turned as Georgia entered the room.

'Lady Willoughby—good evening. To what do I owe this unexpected pleasure?' Georgia regarded her glamorously dressed visitor curiously. Every item of her costume was à la mode, as if she'd stepped right out of the books of a fashion magazine showing off the latest styles from London and Paris. Her wavy red hair reminded Georgia of a Raphaelite model; the auburn locks tucked into a bun under her elaborately decorated hat shone brightly in perfect contrast to her pale, creamy skin.

Lady Willoughby nodded graciously. 'Good evening, Ms Claremont. Please accept my apologies for the uninvited intrusion.'

'Won't you sit down? Would you like some refreshments?' Georgia gestured towards the seating area.

'No, thank you. What I have to say won't take long.'

Georgia tilted her head to the side, perplexed by the odd encounter with Daniel's former lover. 'I'll get to the point, shall I?' Lady Willoughby suggested tightly.

'Please.' Georgia nodded.

'I don't think you should marry Daniel. You're not right for him.' She held up her hand, preventing Georgia's outraged protest. 'Let me explain: I am aware of Daniel's upcoming inheritance. I don't know if you know, but we were once lovers when I was married to my dreadful husband, now, thankfully, with his maker somewhere fiery and hot, I imagine.'

Georgia raised an eyebrow but remained silent. Obviously, she was unaware their engagement had been terminated, but if this rude woman wanted to air her dirty laundry unnecessarily, she might as well let her. At that point, she was on a roll, and it would most likely be impossible to get a word in anyway.

'I've always thought Daniel and I could have made a go of it, given half a chance. I get the feeling your relationship is not a love match. It's all too convenient for my liking.' She viewed Georgia slyly from beneath her long eyelashes.

Georgia remained silent. *Let her dig her own grave,* she thought.

'Do you love him, may I ask?' said Lady Willoughby.

Georgia wondered how she had found out about the inheritance, but she knew even the most obscure news was able to reach the ears of polite society in no time and that servants were a big part of the gossip grapevine.

'Firstly, my feelings for Daniel are really none of your business. Secondly, it's a moot point, as I'm sure you'll be pleased to know that we are no longer betrothed.' Georgia watched with pleasure as Lady Willoughby's mouth fell open in surprise.

She opened her mouth as if to comment.

'No, Lady Willoughby, I do not wish to hear any more from you. You've said quite enough, don't you think? I wish you to leave—now, please,' said Georgia, her hazel grey eyes flashing dangerously.

Lady Willoughby clamped her mouth shut and swept past Georgia and out of the room without another word.

CHAPTER TEN

'You did what?' Daniel looked up at Lady Willoughby from where he was seated at his desk. His anger was palpable.

Lady Willoughby took the seat opposite him. 'Oh, don't start—that woman wasn't right for you, and you know it,' she said haughtily.

'And you are, I suppose?'

'Well, yes.' She watched his face, trying to decipher what he was thinking. 'So, errm ... why did you break it off?'

'It's none of your business, Grace,' Daniel countered.

Lady Willoughby sniffed indignantly. 'That's what she said.'

Daniel attempted to change the subject. 'How's Joanna?'

'She's fine and settling in well,' said Lady Willoughby sullenly.

Daniel regarded her disdainfully. Lady Willoughby was in her mid-thirties, a widow determined to marry without her beautiful, adolescent, spoilt brat of a daughter getting in the way. She had recently returned from Paris, where she'd dropped off poor Joanna at a renowned finishing school for daughters of the well-to-do and gentry. Daniel was all too familiar with Grace's shenanigans, as he was still in touch with her long-suffering, older brother, Willam.

'That ingrate of a husband of mine gambled away most of his fortune and then started on mine. He left us practically destitute. Thankfully, Willam paid for Joanna's tuition. With a bit of luck, I'll be able to get through a successful coming out and find a suitable match when the time comes.'

'So, you'll both be looking for rich husbands, I take it?'

Lady Willoughby sniffed, turned up her nose and gave him a hard look, unamused by his obvious gibe.

'How did you find out about my inheritance, by the way?' Daniel asked.

'Your brother Thomas told me. He thought I could help.'

'How? He knew quite well I was already engaged,' growled Daniel.

'To a coloured woman? Really, Daniel?'

Daniel frowned. 'I don't appreciate your ignorance, Grace.

'Not that it matters, but you do know that her father is white and titled? She grew up just as privileged and in similar circles to you and I. Obviously, in certain circumstances and attitudes, this is no protection when it comes to the matter of race.' Daniel shook his head ruefully.

'Oh, darling, stop being so naïve. How many people in our circles have completely accepted her?'

'Quite a few, actually. Not everyone is as ignorant as you and my interfering brother. Of course, there will always be people like you who think that Black and mixed-heritage people are not suitable for mixing in polite society. It's a good thing not everyone thinks like you.'

Lady Willoughby raised one finely manicured eyebrow. 'I don't have anything against coloureds, I just don't think they fit in certain circles and certainly not as husbands and wives of the gentry. It's absurd.'

'Africans have been mixing with the royal houses of Europe and the gentry for many centuries, Grace. Chattel slavery forced their hands into changing the perception of Africans on this continent in order to justify it. You merely show your ignorance when you make misinformed comments.'

'Oh, you,' Lady Willougby said. 'Always so gracious to outliers within polite society.

'Why did you break up with me? We were good together, and the church would have turned a blind eye, especially with someone of your esteemed background.'

'Grace, I have no intention of marrying you; let me make that clear.' Daniel viewed her sulky mouth and wondered what he had ever seen in the ignorant, spoilt woman. The subject of race and the rights of coloured people in the colonies and ex-colonies had never come up. They never had a reason to discuss any type of serious, thought-provoking subject matter during their tryst. Most of their time had been spent in hotels or in some of the world's high-class gambling clubs in Britain, Paris and New York. Her husband had been too busy with his own mistresses and spending her fortune. He had not cared what his wife got up to once she had given birth to a daughter rather than a son and heir.

Daniel stood. Lady Willoughby jumped from her seat, walked around the desk and placed her hands on his wide shoulders. 'But what about the inheritance?'

'I'll sort something out.' He gently removed her hands from his shoulders.

Grace examined him closely. 'I'll always be fond of you, you must know that—we've known each other forever. I'm sure you'll have no problem finding someone else to marry—you're still a handsome man and no longer a rake. I much preferred you when you were a rake, Daniel. You've turned into a serious bore.' She put her lace gloves on huffily.

'And you're an obnoxious troublemaker. How dare you approach Georgia? You had no right. What must she think?'

'What must she think? You love her, don't you?' Grace stared up into his striking blue eyes.

'I see the hurt in your eyes. You can't hide your feelings from me, Daniel. I've known you since we were children, remember?' She took hold of his chin. 'Have you told her?'

Daniel looked away, turned to the window and shook his head.

'Don't be a fool, Daniel. Let her know how you feel.'

'Why? She doesn't feel the same way. Anyhow, you've suddenly changed your tune.' Daniel glanced at her pessimistically.

Grace smiled wisely. 'This changes everything. Have you even asked her how she feels about you?'

Daniel shook his head crossly, losing patience with her line of questioning.

Lady Willoughby ignored him and leaned conspiratorially towards him. 'Right, now, listen to me.'

Dear Georgia,

I won't beat around the bush—I miss you.

You know I'm not exactly a hopeless romantic, but when I think of you, I think of the words of love expressed in Songs of Solomon. *Are those words enough to express my deep love and respect for you? I hope so.*

I also suspect we might be on the same page—can we start again? Would you give me permission to start off on the right foot and court you the way you deserve? I want to get it right this time round, if you can find it in your heart to give me the opportunity to repair my clumsy attempt at romancing you.

With love, your dearest, Daniel

Georgia's eyes fluttered closed as she savoured her thoughts and feelings about the powerful words in Daniel's letter. *This changes everything!*

With a beatific smile on her face, she read it again and again.

Pushing herself up from the window seat in her apartments, she proceeded to gather her outer garments to let Daniel know her response in person.

She ran down the stairs in a most unladylike manner, resisting the temptation to slide down the banister, grinning as a flashback from her errant schooldays came to mind. She briefly checked her reflection in the hall mirror, opened the front door and gasped as she came face to face with Daniel. Her eyes widened as she noted the bundle in his arms. She brought her hand to her mouth and reached out as baby Nicholas recognised her, gurgled and stretched out his arms.

'How?' Georgia buried her nose in the baby's neck.

'His mother found out she's expecting a child. Her ingrate of a husband is elated and decided that one child in the household was more than enough for him.'

'And what if she changes her mind again?' Georgia's eyes shone with grateful tears as she gazed up at the man she loved.

'Don't worry. I had a solicitor friend draw up some initial paperwork. He is our official ward. You just need to sign your section.' Daniel smiled down at Georgia and baby Nicholas, whose large brown eyes stared happily from one of them to the other.

He cupped Georgia's face.

'I loved your letter,' said Georgia shyly.

'Do you love me as much?'

'Yes.'

Daniel grinned happily. 'Enough to marry me?'

'Yes, I do.' She nodded her head, stood on tiptoes, and leaned in to kiss him.

'Not in front of the child, dear Georgia. Save that for after the ceremony.'

Georgia rolled her eyes, and they laughed joyously as Daniel wrapped his strong arms around his new family.

The End.

ABOUT THE AUTHOR

S. N. Clayton was born and raised in North London. She is a business educator, author, speaker, and avid reader of many genres. Her love for romantic sagas and historical romance fiction began in her early teens when her late mother unknowingly introduced her to Mills & Boon by not reading her library books quickly enough.

Passionate about bridging the gap and showcasing the multicultural history of Britain from an authentic perspective, S. N. Clayton found her first novel in this trilogy, *A Shared History*, both an exciting and challenging project, particularly in terms of research.

She is due to publish the second book in the series, *A Shared Destiny*, in Autumn 2025, which continues the story in Victorian London. The third book, *A Shared*

Promise, takes readers on an adventure across the seas to 1800s New York and the Black West of America. These later books have proven just as fascinating to research. To reflect the depth of her meticulous historical study, S. N. Clayton has also included a recommended book list.

S. N. Clayton lives in Greater London. She currently works as a learning specialist in the commercial field of learning and development and writes part-time.

www.snclayton.com

Twitter: @MicroBizSNC

FURTHER READING – BOOK LIST

- *Staying Power: The History of Black People in Britain* – Peter Fryer
- *How to be a Victorian* – Ruth Goodman
- *Black and British: A Forgotten History* – David Olusoga
- *Black Americans in Victorian Britain* – Jeffrey Green
- *Black Jacks: African American Seamen in the Age of Sail* – W Jeffrey Bolster
- *Black Gotham: A Family History of African Americans in Nineteenth-Century New York City* – Carla L Peterson
- *Before Harlem: The Black Experience in New York City Before World War I* – Marcy S Sacks
- *Classic Jamaican Cooking* – Caroline Sullivan

Conscious Dreams
PUBLISHING

Transforming diverse writers
into successful published authors

www.consciousdreamspublishing.com

authors@consciousdreamspublishing.com

Let's connect